NOT QUITE SO STORIES

David S. Atkinson

For Brett —
Thanks for all the help!

Literary Wanderlust LLC | Denver

Published in the United States by Literary Wanderlust LLC, Denver, Colorado.

www.LiteraryWanderlust.com

Library of Congress Control Number: 2015949909

ISBN print 978-1-942856-03-0
ISBN digital 978-1-942856-04-7

Cover design: Ruth M'Gonigle

Printed in the United States of America

Dedication

For Shannon, who graciously puts up with my absurdities and loves
me anyway.

Also for every third person named Fred.

.

Acknowledgements

I have so many people I need to thank for this book seeing the light of day. There is no way with my flawed brain that I am going to be able to remember them all. I should go ahead and give up my present way of life to become a yogurt farmer in Northern Duluth, because that's really the only course available to me in my shame that I will forget someone.

Regardless, Susan Brooks and Linda Joffe Hull have to be at the top of the list. Susan's belief in this book is something I will never be able to repay, and I'd be just as lost if Linda hadn't suggested I send this book to Susan. Thank you both from the bottom of my heart.

I also want to thank all the people who read these stories and gave me feedback over the years as I worked on them. These stories took a long time to fully develop, and I couldn't have done it without each and every person along the way. Joseph Michael Owens, Nissa Pearson (Wallinga at the time), Trevor Alexander, John Domini, Karolyn Sherwood, Stephanie Austin, Jerry VanIeperen, Denise Emanuel Clemen, Chris Smith, AE Stueve, and Bill Howard James, you guys are all the best. Each of you. All at once.

But I can't forget the journals that originally published some of these stories, and all the wonderful people who read those journals and said such nice things to me about the stories. Thank you all for believing in my writing. Your support and encouragement along the way really kept me going.

Last but not least, I want to thank all the writers who have given me such good things to read and taught me what kinds of things are possible. Etgar Keret, Amelia Gray, George Saunders,

3

Aimee Bender, and so on way beyond the space I have here. Wonderful stuff all.

There are so many people to thank. No one writes in a vacuum. Thank goodness I don't live in one.

Before he became a hermit, Zarathud was a young Priest, and took great delight in making fools of his opponents in front of his followers.

One day Zarathud took his students to a pleasant pasture and there he confronted The Sacred Chao while she was contentedly grazing.

"Tell me, you dumb beast," demanded the Priest in his commanding voice, "why don't you do something worthwhile. What is your Purpose in Life, anyway?"

Munching the tasty grass, The Sacred Chao replied "MU."*

Upon hearing this, absolutely nobody was enlightened. Primarily because nobody could understand Chinese.

—"Zarathud's Enlightenment," *Principia Discordia*

*MU is the Chinese ideogram for NO-THING

Contents

G-MEN

Broderick surveyed his airmen's brushed-metal chronograph wristwatch. Four twenty-seven and thirty-six seconds. He tapped the toe of his black paratrooper boot impatiently. The tapping clanged on the studded metal floor of the hangar. Only one last jumper to screen. Then the workday finished and he could go home.

The clanging from his tapping toe echoed around the corrugated tin walls of the large hangar. Not that hangar one forty-three was any larger than any of the other SSA hangars; they were all identical. The sound would have echoed in any of them.

Four twenty-seven and fifty-seven seconds, Broderick noted. He stood in front of the rigid metal strip bench, clipboard in hand, ready for the moment the jumper appeared. The bench was all the way at one end of the hangar, but Broderick did not wander around. An official member of the SSA should be the first thing the jumper saw upon arrival.

Broderick shifted in the straps of his canvas jumpsuit, a bit stiff from standing in his authority pose. His pack felt heavier the longer he waited, making him want to roll his shoulders. He refrained, however. It was more important to be sure that the right impression was conveyed. Four-twenty-nine and seventeen seconds.

He had already processed fourteen jumpers that day. The next would be number fifteen. Broderick processed fifteen jumpers during every workday, all SSA officers did. Each screening was allocated thirty minutes by regulation. A half-hour each day for mandated breaks and an hour for scheduled lunch came up to a full nine-hour shift.

Broderick frowned. His chronograph wristwatch read four-thirty-one and sixteen seconds. That meant a daredevil jumper. If the jumper pulled his cord at exactly six thousand feet, he would have arrived at exactly four thirty. Over-cautious ones pulled before six thousand worried they'd do it too late and get hurt, and arrived early. Daredevils pushed opening their chute to the last moment, trying to get just a few more seconds of free-fall time, waiting as long as they could stomach it, risking hitting the ground too fast, before panic set in and they pulled.

Joe Kreller; twenty-six, financial analyst, red hair, Broderick read off the sheet attached to his clipboard. He knew the type. The jumper was quite a bit younger than Broderick. That red hair was probably a full head, not like Broderick's thin wispy brown remnants. He imagined the slick young professional whooping one last weekend warrior yell before going for his chute.

Broderick readied himself, even though he was already ready. The jumper was a daredevil, but he'd pull eventually. A couple of seconds at most. There were different types of jumpers, but each type was predictable. This one too.

Of course, the jumper technically wouldn't pull his chute. Not quite. SSA procedure stated that jumpers were to be stopped immediately prior to actual parachute deployment just as they were about to pull. There had been incidents before implementation of that rule. Quite a mess, with parachute all over the hangar, and repacking required before the next jumper could be processed. However, things weren't done in that fashion anymore. This one would not have pulled.

Sure enough, at four-thirty-one and fifty-five seconds, Broderick saw the air shimmer on the bench, indicating a transport in progress. He stood up even straighter. Rigid, appropriate for an officer.

Suddenly the jumper was there, sitting on the bench where the air shimmer had indicated. And suddenly, or at least it seemed that way to Broderick, the jumper was a woman. A woman with startlingly red hair, appropriate since Broderick was startled, tied back in a bouncy ponytail. Red like he remembered Samantha's hair being before she left. Apparently Joe must have been a nickname for Josephine or some such thing and the paperwork failed to note it. The jumper's eyes were wide and shocky, her moment of realization imminent.

"Ta-da!" Broderick threw open his arms, recovering himself as fast as he could from his surprise, holding carefully onto the clipboard. The jumper flinched back and almost fell backward over the bench.

The ta-da wasn't strictly procedure. Not exactly. Broderick came up with it on his own, though he kept meaning to suggest official SSA adoption of the technique. He found the ta-da helpful. Jumpers weren't as likely to meltdown at abruptly finding themselves sitting in a hangar when they'd been falling at a hundred miles an hour through nothing the moment before. Perhaps it distracted them from trying to understand what had happened and kept the animal portion of their brains from having to come up with an explanation. Regardless, fewer incidents occurred after he first tried out the ta-da, so Broderick continued the practice.

The jumper stared at Broderick, her eyes piercingly wild, as if Broderick might be a snake coiled to attack. Her long fingers gripped the edge of the bench tightly as if they were the only things holding her securely there. Not so different from all the other jumpers.

"What the—"

"Miss Joe Kreller," Broderick snapped, cutting off the jumper as soon as she spoke. Broderick always did that was well. However, that was part of procedure. The irritation from interruption was supposed to make jumpers forget the oddity of their situation, make things seem more normal.

"Where the hell—"

"Are you or are you not Joe Kreller?" Broderick demanded, interrupting the jumper again. He didn't even have to listen for her to start talking again before he performed the mandated second interruption. Anymore, Broderick just found himself interrupting right at the correct spot by reflex.

"Yes. Now where the hell am I?" The jumper threw up her arms as she yelled. Then she grabbed the bench again swiftly, her eyes darting nervously.

Broderick let the jumper finish this time. It was okay. The SSA procedure manual required two interruptions. Once the requirement was fulfilled, the SSA officer performing inspection was allowed to provide requested explanations. Broderick flipped the metal cover on the clipboard closed.

"You are in hangar one-forty-three of SSA facility Alpha," he informed her with a pleased smile. "As a jumper, you have been detained for a routine screening. Nothing out of the ordinary. If you cooperate and check out, then we should have you falling again shortly."

"SSA?"

"Skydiving Security Administration. We're a sub-department of Homeland Security. Like the Transportation Security Administration, but for skydiving. We're separate since jumping isn't really transportation."

Broderick smiled again like he remembered smiling at Samantha while waiting for her to finish ranting about how they never did anything more interesting than hanging out and watching television. A friendly disposition on the part of SSA officers, once authority was established, encouraged compliance, at least according to the manual. Broderick was concerned, though. The jumper twitched a good deal, looking around like a mouse caught in the middle of the kitchen floor when the light just came on.

"But I was just midair. How did I get here?"

Broderick forced himself to keep the smile. "Jumpers are detained mid-jump to ensure that they might not have accepted explosives or other unauthorized cargo after deplaning," he patiently recited the scripted explanation. "Such cargo could be obtained from another jumper or some such midair source. Besides, if inspections were performed pre-takeoff, then jumpers from planes that snuck across the border would still be a risk. Thus, policy requires detainment must occur during descent."

"Explosives," the jumper sputtered. "But *how* did I get here?"

The smile went a little tight-lipped despite Broderick's best efforts. "The acquisition process specifics are sensitive information," he replied. "Don't you worry, though. We can do it. You're here, aren't you?"

Broderick bluffed. Not that the technology of the acquisition process wasn't sensitive information. It was. However, procedure allowed SSA officers to provide redacted step-throughs when asked. These were allowed, not required. Acquisition specifics are the job of the grunts down in tech as far as Broderick was concerned. SSA officers had more important tasks to handle.

"How haven't I heard about this before?" The jumper raised one gracefully plucked eyebrow, just visible under the helmet. "Something like this should be all over the news."

Broderick crossed his arms, clipboard still in one hand. "Well, inspections aren't exactly the highlight of you guys' trips, are they?

Probably not what you'd want to gush about to the other guys back on the ground. Besides, it doesn't make the stupid hobby seem quite so death defying if somebody could snatch you up safely at any time. I guess your jumper friends don't want anyone to think about that."

Broderick paused, waiting for the jumper to shoot something back. They usually did when their *sport* was slighted. That was fine. Again, procedure. Used when jumpers started dragging out inspections with unnecessary questions.

"So," Broderick continued, "once we get you processed you can get back to all that." He smiled again, hoping it wasn't coming off as a sneer. Samantha had sometimes taken his smile as a sneer.

"Fine." The jumper scowled. "What do you want?"

"Identity verification. I've already completed the visual evaluation of your person for explosives and other terrorist devices. You're clean on that front. Once we verify your identity you can proceed with your jump."

"Proceed?" The jumper raised both eyebrows that time, but less shocked than mocking. Too mocking to remind Broderick of a mouse anymore. Much more like Samantha toward the end. "How am I going to do that since I'm already on the ground?"

Broderick sighed, rolling his eyes to emphasize the idiocy of the question. "Once the inspection is complete, I will clear you to continue and open the hangar door." He gestured with the clipboard at the far end of the hanger. "Exiting through the opening will drop you approximately one thousand feet above your point of detainment acquisition. To continue your falling from there you simply have to fall."

The jumper stared at the end of the hangar for a moment. Then she looked back at Broderick. "Okay, so how do you verify who I am? Body scan or something?"

Broderick tapped the toe of his black paratrooper boot again. The echo of the hollow clang on the studded metal floor was satisfying. It eased the irritation a bit. "We start with your ID."

The jumper started unbuckling the clasps of her curve-hugging spandex skydiving suit to get at her pants pocket inside. "Sure. What would you have done if I hadn't had it with me? Not like I thought I was exactly going to need it."

Broderick snatched the jumper's ID irritably from her outstretched hand. "We would proceed as necessary until we could verify you," he snapped. "Fingerprints, DNA, whatever we had to do. Otherwise," he gestured again, "that hangar door doesn't open."

The jumper folded her arms but didn't say anything more, a classic Samantha move.

Holding the ID up so he could see the photo and the jumper at the same time, Broderick compared. Well, he pretended to. He knew right away that it was the jumper's real ID; he'd read her chart. She was a young woman out for a thrill, not a conspirator. Still, jumpers got difficult if officers didn't stick to the script.

"It's me."

Broderick looked a little longer. "Right," he muttered, nodding his head once decisively. Then he walked over to steel panel on the corrugated sheet metal wall. He banged on it with a fist and it slid open with a grinding noise. It was not open enough to see what was on the other side. Broderick inserted the ID and the steel panel slammed shut.

"I know it's a pain," he told the jumper.

Procedure stated SSA officers were to attempt *buddying* up to jumpers while IDs were authenticated and identities were cross-referenced in the federal databases. A substantial amount of time could be required for that portion of the process and jumpers had a tendency to get agitated when not kept mentally busy by an at least perceived sympathetic interest. They just needed someone to commiserate with, studies showed.

"No one likes the hassle, but it's the price of safety. Prevents the terrorists from dropping down on us from the skies on big old parachutes with dynamite strapped to their chests."

Broderick turned around to face the jumper, to add a little face-to-face to the buddying, but she just sagged on the bench with her pretty helmeted head held in her hands. That signaled trouble. It wasn't the reaction of camaraderic commiseration against bureaucracy that was intended by the conveyed appearance of sympathetic interest. Broderick frowned.

"Hey," he reassured her, "it won't be long now. Believe me, I want to get this over with as much as you. I need to get home to catch a season finale. I've waited all year to see it."

"You guys ruin it. You just ruin the whole thing," the jumper moaned. Her head was still down.

"Ruin?" Broderick checked his chronograph wristwatch. Four-fifty-two and thirty-four seconds. The wristwatch also contained a device for transferring problem jumpers to containment cells. All he had to do was push.

"This is the freest thing possible and you cut it up and contain it into useless little pieces." The jumper's head shot up and she waved her hands all around, but not violently so Broderick took his thumb off the button. "What's the point of it now? There isn't one if you're going to do all this to it."

"Come on," Broderick countered, actually feeling sympathy for once. This was almost word for word what Samantha had said in that last argument. "It isn't that bad. You still get to do your falling. Even some extra because we dump you higher up than where we grabbed you. All you have to do is sit and wait a little in the middle. It's still the same."

"The same? Are you crazy?" The jumper's eyes blazed passionately at Broderick. "When you're up there like that, careening toward the ground with nothing to stop you, everything past and future is ripped away. Adrenaline leaps on you and you can't conceive of anything other than the specific, overwhelming present. Pure fear on a body level. For once in your stinking life you're completely alive. Alive and in the moment. Nothing else is real at that point."

The jumper's head fell back into her hands. Broderick was too stunned to respond.

"And this smashes that all to pieces." The jumper shook her head limply. "It sucks the life right out. No different than waiting in line at the bank."

Broderick swallowed. She even sounded like Samantha.

"Not like you don't know," the jumper waved a hand feebly at Broderick without looking at him. "I'm sure you've felt how different it is now."

Broderick stared. "Um. I haven't actually ever jumped. It wasn't required for the job."

The jumper's head shot up again, her crystal-blue eyes as wide as the hangar. "What? But the getup, the parachute."

Broderick fingered the straps of his pack where they crisscrossed over the front of his canvas jumpsuit. "It's just a safety precaution. All SSA officers wear them, in case we get sucked out when the hangar door opens."

"Unbelievable," the jumper muttered. Her jaw hung slack. "No wonder you can do this. You just have no idea what you're doing."

"I mean," Broderick stammered, "it's not like I don't know how. I know all about it. SSA officers pass a jump course. Just in case. We just don't have to actually do a jump."

The jumper shook her head. "No one who knew would have anything to do with this. Not the slightest thing."

Broderick tried to think of a retort, something to come back with. He couldn't think of anything, though. He hadn't been able to when Samantha walked out either.

The steel panel clanged open again. Broderick flinched. He'd forgotten all about it. The jumper's ID stuck out the opening made by the open panel.

Broderick walked over and grabbed the ID. He handed it back to the jumper without looking at her. Then Broderick flipped open the clipboard and scribbled something unimportant.

"You check out," he tried to say enthusiastically like it should make the jumper happy. He knew it wouldn't, though. "You can be on your way." He walked over and hit a large red button on the wall. The button clicked in and a siren wailed through the hangar. At the other end, the steel door swung outward, slowly. Sunlight shot in.

"Go on," Broderick ordered, trying to still sound authoritative even though he no longer felt it. "Finish your jump."

"Whatever," the jumper muttered, not getting up off the bench.

"You might as well go out that way." Broderick pointed at the raising hangar door. "You won't like the other way out of here."

The jumper shrugged and got to her feet, shuffling toward the open door. Broderick followed.

When the jumper got to the edge, she looked out. Broderick looked too, seeing the empty space below the lip of the hangar floor. Far below, the ground was tiny having been partitioned into mowed flat squares in various shades of green and brown stretching out endlessly. Probably farmland. Kansas or something like that.

The jumper looked at Broderick and Broderick looked back at her. It seemed like the jumper was about to say something, but then she shrugged and just walked off the edge. Not jumped, just sort of stepped out. She drifted under the lip as she fell, causing Broderick to lose sight of her.

"You still got your jump," Broderick mumbled to no one. He stared at all that flat ground way down below. The hangar door began the slow process of swinging closed.

A voice whispered to Broderick as he stood at the edge, the jumper's voice, or perhaps Samantha's, that SSA officers were the only ones who could get around screening for jumps. An officer could sneak out after a jumper cleared and everyone would think freak winds sucked him out. An accident. There wouldn't even be a reprimand, much less an arrest. It was the only chance anyone had to go for real.

Broderick's knees buckled, a reflex shiver shooting through his body as he imagined the physical sensation of jumping before the door closed, and he gripped the corrugated sheet metal wall. No, that sort of thing wasn't for him. That's what he'd told Samantha though they hadn't been talking about skydiving then. He just wanted to get home and watch some TV.

But then, almost like a flinch, Broderick's body leaped forward. The jump he'd never made with Samantha. Forward out into the open air, past the confines of the hangar, out over the green and brown patchwork ground somewhere way down below.

CENTS OF WONDER RHYMES WITH ORANGE

The young blond man in the wrinkled oxford shirt dashed across the tile of the elevator lobby. Hurrying, his hands juggled a laptop satchel, a dry and folded umbrella, and a lumpy plastic grocery bag. Lunging for the elevator button before managing to stop, the sole of his cheap dress shoe slid out from under him and he slipped quickly, and clumsily, to the floor.

An orange popped out of the grocery bag and rolled away as he hit. At first, the young man struggled to get up and catch the orange, but he stopped and watched as it proceeded up a wheelchair ramp next to a small set of stairs. It went all the way up the ramp and came to a rest just over the top.

"Huh," the young man mumbled, propped up on his side by his left elbow. "That was weird."

"Goodness. Are you all right?"

An older, frumpy woman, whitening brown hair heaped in a massive bun, waddled into the lobby. The squatty heels of her thick clogs clacked on the shiny tiles as she shambled over, bearing a cardboard filing box.

"Yeah," he said, glancing back at the orange. "I mean, yes, I'm fine, thanks. I just slipped." He heaved himself up off the floor and dusted himself off.

"You have to be more careful," she clucked, seeing that he wasn't hurt. Shifting the box onto a good-sized hip, she went on, "These floors are slick when they've been waxed."

"Did you see that?" He pointed at the orange. He walked over, grabbed the offending orb, and held it up. "It ran up."

"Must've missed that. All I saw was you on the floor." She smiled. "Maybe it was just from how hard you hit the ground."

"No. It didn't hit that hard," he insisted.

As if for emphasis, he dropped the orange to the tile. The orange hit with a *thud* sound and stopped. Then, slowly, it began to roll. The young man and the frump watched silently as it methodically moved its way across the floor back to the same spot from where the young man had just fetched it.

"Told you."

"Well," the older woman exclaimed, setting down the file box. "There's something you don't see every day."

The young man ran and grabbed the orange again. He stopped and looked carefully around the floor and ramp. Then he held up the orange and examined it as well.

"Maybe the floor isn't even," she suggested, placing a hand on her cheek. "Maybe it just looks uphill when it really isn't, an optical illusion."

"Nope." The young man bent down and scanned where the ramp met the rest of the floor. "It runs uphill all right."

The woman pursed her lips and put her hands on her sides. They both stood and regarded the floor. The young man rolled the orange around in his hand.

Squeaking wheels caused them both to glance up as a mustached delivery man in coveralls pushed a hand truck loaded with packages into the lobby. He nodded at them each in turn, tipping an imaginary cap, and reached for the elevator button.

Smiling at the woman, the young man raised the orange high into the air and then let go. As it dropped, the delivery man raised an eyebrow. The older woman and younger man looked back and then watched as the delivery man's gaze turned to watch the orange work its way up the wheelchair ramp.

Once the orange stopped, the delivery man exhaled sharply. "Now that's a neat trick. How'd you get it to do that?"

The young man shrugged. "We didn't do anything. *It's* doing it on *its* own."

The woman nodded in agreement.

"You don't say." The delivery man tilted the hand truck upright. "All by itself?"

"Do it again," the older woman urged excitedly. "Show him."

Eagerly, the young man obeyed. The woman and the delivery man stared as the young man grabbed the orange and plopped it in the same spot. Predictably, the orange again came to a stop at the top of the ramp. All three clapped.

"What's making it do that?" The delivery man asked no one in particular as he ran his fingers through his mustache.

"I can't figure it out," the young man replied. "I'm stumped." He turned to the woman, but she just shrugged her shoulders and laughed.

"Suppose you put something in the way," the delivery man suggested. "So it can't go? What do you think'll happen then?"

The woman and young man looked at each other, but neither answered. The woman pointed at her file box and the young man pushed it over in front of the ramp. Then they all held their breath as the young man dropped the orange again.

Sure enough, the orange began to move along the exact same path as the other times. However, when it reached the file box, it stopped.

"Aww," the young man and delivery man sighed in unison.

"Wait," the woman cried. "Look."

Very slowly, the orange moved forward. The file box began to move as well, propelled by the orange. Though not as fast as before, the orange pushed the file box to the top of the wheelchair ramp. Then, for no more apparent reason than any of the other times, it stopped again.

"Yeah," the delivery man shouted. "Look at that."

Suddenly, a surly little man in an immaculately pressed pinstripe suit stormed into the lobby. His black hair was combed back in a wave, puffed several inches high on his head.

"What the hell are you people doing?" he demanded gruffly. His pointer finger jabbed sharply at the elevator button.

"It's this orange," the young man excitedly explained. "Every time we drop it, the thing goes uphill. We can't figure it out. It's amazing."

"Sure is," the delivery man chimed in. "It can't be doing it, but it is. Damnedest thing. It even pushed that box along with it."

"So what?" The elevator doors opened and the angry little man charged inside. He spun around and, just before the elevator doors closed, demanded, "Don't you people have jobs to go to?"

For a moment, the three stood in place. They sheepishly glanced around at each other. The young man shuffled his feet. The delivery man cleared his throat.

"Well then," the older woman finally remarked, adjusting her bun. She pressed the call button and hefted her file box. The delivery man tilted the hand truck and started pushing it toward the elevators. The young man retrieved the orange and stuffed it back into the grocery bag. When the doors opened, they went inside.

DOMESTIC TIES

Charlotte pumped her arm in circular motions, hunched over the antique coffee table to put as much pressure as possible between the polishing cloth and the darkly shining mahogany surface. That was the only way to ensure that the table gleamed. Force the wax into the grain. The table needed to reflect like lacquer. The prisoner would be coming soon.

The shine faded fast. Dust collected daily. Even as time simply passed, a certain dullness crept in. A cozy would have been easier. Protect the surface with no polishing at all, but the table was an heirloom. It had to be polished and displayed.

She rose and stood back to survey the light reflecting off the coffee table, hands resting on the hips of her light blue cotton dress. Tilting her head, she checked different angles. Then she rotated around the table to verify the uniformity of the wax. Finally satisfied, she nodded. It was as a mirror.

The sunlight shone softly on the table top through the freshly laundered lace curtains. Charlotte approved. The living room was almost presentable. The other rooms already were. Even if her home would house a prisoner, at least it was in respectable shape.

Except for the carpet. Exactly three days had passed since the cream Berber was vacuumed. Charlotte vacuumed exactly every three days. Really, she wanted to do it daily. To be tidy. However, daily vacuuming wore good carpet out too quickly. Three days kept the Berber from wearing but still allowed her to keep it free from

15

dirt. Two days had passed, though. It was time for the carpet to be cleaned.

Hurrying through the dining room, with the walnut dining table and freshly washed place settings arranged for the evening meal, Charlotte fetched the reliable metal vacuum cleaner from its closet in the kitchen. Not cheap plastic like the worthless more modern models that threw more dust than they picked up. No. This white and beige workhorse had been her mother's. Her mother used it for years before she passed, making sure Charlotte understood the difference a good vacuum cleaner made in a house.

The vacuum cleaner roared to life at Charlotte's instruction and she shouldered it around the living room in circles of decreasing size. Of course, she carefully and gingerly circumnavigated the furniture inhabiting the room to avoid knocking anything askew. Then, after pausing for any possible dust kicked up to become complacent and settle, Charlotte repeated the task in the opposite direction. Once satisfied that all marks in the carpet were erased, Charlotte returned the vacuum cleaner to its post in the kitchen closet to silently await its next duty.

She paused to take a breath after she sealed the closet door, but just then the grandfather clock in the dining room sounded. She immediately recalled the next chores to be performed, but she chided herself. The schedule would have to adapt, she reminded herself since a prisoner was due to arrive.

The letter of notification was on the kitchen table, by itself. Charlotte placed it there when she reread it that morning after Ward whistled his way off to work. She reread it again and again, just to make sure she understood. That she had it all right.

The paper itself was a printed form letter. Only her and Ward's information and the specifics had been added in blanks by a typewriter.

As run of the mill as a jury duty notice, only it notified that the state would be requisitioning the use of her home for the purpose of providing shelter to a convict. *The prisons were impossibly overcrowded*, the letter informed. *Unable to determine any other immediate solution, the state had no choice but to place prisoners in private residences.*

Charlotte looked at that portion of the letter again, still sure she must have mistaken the contents somehow. *The measure was temporary*, the letter assured. *Citizens were chosen for the duty randomly in order to assure a fair distribution of the burden and each citizen only had to bear the burden for a month. Then, another home would be randomly chosen. The entire program would immediately cease as soon as an expansion prison could be built. This inconvenience,* the letter explained, *was a necessary obligation for the maintenance of a free state.*

Charlotte carefully placed the letter back on the kitchen table. Then she dashed to the hutch for a tumbler before hurrying to the refrigerator to fix herself an iced tea.

The coolness of the iced tea and the clink of the glass tumbler on her lower teeth calmed Charlotte. She took a light breath and exhaled. Then she straightened the collar of her dress and took another sip.

She thought the letter a mistake or possibly a joke when it first arrived. The idea was preposterous, putting prisoners in respectable homes. It had never been done. At least, she had never heard of such a thing. However, Ward only nodded, chewing his roast, when she scoffed at the matter during dinner. He'd heard about the situation at his office. It was real, all of the sales department talked about it. The overcrowding at the prison sure was a real problem.

She was sure it was a problem, she told him, but in her home? What if something happened to her? This was a convicted criminal, a dangerous man. She could be attacked.

Ward chuckled at this. He was sure the state took appropriate measures to ensure safety. They wouldn't implement the program if they could not be sure of safety. He said she was worrying about nothing.

That was easy for him to say. He didn't have to stay at home with the prisoner. He went to work all day. There was no need for him to worry, but things were different for her. She stayed at home all day. All day with a prisoner.

Ward just sat back, digesting his potatoes, and pointed out that she didn't have to sit around the house either. Not if she didn't want to. Heck, it wasn't like they had any children to fuss over. She could spend the day shopping. Or, take some of those courses down at the community center. Hadn't he even said she could get her real estate agent license when she said she was bored that time? Yes, she should do that.

Charlotte sighed, remembering. She finished the iced tea and rinsed the tumbler in the sink. Then she turned on the water hot, squeezed detergent from the bottle waiting there, and scrubbed the tumbler clean. After she dried the glass with the cloth hanging from the cabinet door in front of the sink, she paused to let the air absorb any remaining moisture before replacing the tumbler in the hutch.

That was Ward. He didn't understand. If she spent her days gallivanting all over town, then the housework would never get done. The whole day was required. She couldn't just fritter time away taking courses or amusing herself.

Ward always said he would help around the house. That she shouldn't finish everything before he got home.

She shook her head. Ward was sweet, but sometimes a bit clueless. He was tired at the end of the long workday and needed the chance to relax. Otherwise, he wouldn't be fresh for work the next day. There would be no more promotions because he'd be too worn out to distinguish himself. Then where would they be? No, as nice as help would be, Charlotte knew he needed to focus himself, first and foremost, on his job. That left the housework to her.

Charlotte started as the doorbell suddenly rang. She swallowed dryly. Normally, it was such a happy tune, announcing a visitor to briefly interrupt the monotony of the morning. This, however, was surely the prisoner. This time, the chime felt more like an air raid siren.

Well, there was nothing to do about it. She just had to accept matters and smile. This would happen. She straightened her dress and hair, ensuring she was appropriately presentable. Then she marched briskly through the dining room into the foyer and opened the cherry wood front door with the frosted panes of glass separated into a pretty pattern by connecting lines of lead.

"Howdy," a heavy man in a tan uniform bellowed out pleasantly the moment Charlotte opened the door. She noticed that his light brown shirt, starched, with the silver badge on the breast, bulged over his belly and was tucked haphazardly into his darker brown pants. His thumbs hooked into the pockets just drew her focus more toward the sloppiness of the tucking around his belly. He unhooked one of his thumbs and used it to tip the front of his cowboy-ish hat in an apparent attempt at a polite gesture.

"Got your criminal here," the heavy man went on, shoving a little mouse of a man dressed in an orange coverall suit through the doorway without further introduction. "All ready for you."

Charlotte jumped, not expecting the prisoner to just barge right in like that. What if the guard had got the wrong house? He got right down to it. No pleasantries or anything.

The little man in orange stumbled from the shove, apparently not expecting the guard's haste either. There were handcuffs on his hands and feet and a little chain running between like Charlotte could just hang him on the coat rack by the door and be done. When he recovered his balance, the prisoner did not look at her or the home in which he was to be lodged. Perhaps he was not curious. Instead, he looked at his plain brown clunky shoes. His shoulders had fallen like he had a sack of wet clothes on his back. Charlotte found herself staring at the bald spot on his little head, facing her, and ringed by wispy gray hair remnants.

"Oh," Charlotte exclaimed, recovering herself enough to remember decorum. "Do come in. Of course, come in."

"Thank you kindly," the heavy man blustered as he rolled inside past her, shoving to keep the little man stumbling ahead. Charlotte quickly shut the front door and hurried to catch up as the guard and the little prisoner continued that way into the dining room.

"Nice spread," the heavy man puffed, looking around almost like he expected highwaymen to be hiding behind the furniture. "Any little ones?"

"No," she replied. "Ward and I—"

"Kitchen'll be the best place then," the heavy man interrupted. He began shoving the little man in that direction without further delay. "Should be out of you folks' way pretty good in there."

"The kitchen?" Charlotte could not imagine this man thought her kitchen an appropriate place to keep a prisoner. She hurried after him, though, since he shoved the little man in there.

"Yep," the heavy man concluded, surveying the room while nodding. The prisoner stood quietly next to the kitchen table in his orange coverall suit, looking down at the floor. "This'll do fine."

"The kitchen?" Charlotte repeated. "I need my kitchen. Wouldn't the basement be more suitable? Or perhaps the garage?"

"Nah." The heavy man quickly dismissed her concern, taking a black oil chalk wrapped in rough brown paper out of a pocket. "This here little guy won't take up much room. Besides, I expect you'll probably want him where you can keep an eye on him."

He shoved the little man to an out of the way spot of the floor. Then he started drawing a big square around him. The prisoner just stood there, shuffling a little. The black oil chalk left a horrible looking mark on the floor. Dark and dirty compared to the nicely waxed white linoleum.

"Wait a moment," Charlotte protested when she realized what was happening. "My floor."

"Aww, don't worry none," the heavy man reassured her with a tone that sounded just a bit too patronizing to Charlotte. "He's gotta know where his limits are, and this'll wash off with a little elbow grease later on."

Charlotte's indignation deflated. She knew she really would have no trouble cleaning the mark later, ugly as it was for the moment. The heavy man was right. The heavy man? She still didn't know his name, or the prisoner's for that matter. Regardless, the black mark would disappear with cleanser and scrubbing. But why have it at all? What would that terrible mark accomplish?

The guard finished drawing the square and struggled back to his feet, puffing with the exertion. His face turned red. He put the oil chalk back in his pocket and hiked up his dark brown stiff pants.

"There now," he commented, apparently to no one in particular. "You behave now," he said to the prisoner. "Hear?"

The little man didn't acknowledge the instruction. Instead, he continued staring at his shoes. Motionless, more like a prisoner's statue. Charlotte noticed that the orange coveralls were several sizes too large for him, like a boy dressed up in his father's suit. Surely the state could find prisoners clothing that fit, couldn't they?

"Well," the guard interrupted Charlotte's thoughts, "I should be on my way. Ma'am," he said, touching his thumb to his hat brim again, before turning and walking out of the room toward the front door.

Charlotte blinked. Then, a moment later, she chased after him, catching him in the dining room.

"Wait," she pleaded, clutching at his arm. "You are leaving? What about the prisoner?"

"Shoot," the guard laughed. "You don't need to worry none about him. He'll stay in his box like he's been told. I'm sure you folks can manage. Just don't let him balance your checkbook and you'll be fine."

"But. . . but. . ." she stammered, "who is going to guard him?"

The guard shook his head. "That one doesn't need any guard," he chuckled. "Just let him be. Someone'll be around each morning to take him to the shower and can. Bring him food and duds and all that. Other than that, he ain't no different than a plant. Just sits and *pho-to-sin-thee-sizes* and whatnot till his sentence is served."

Charlotte stared. Was he just going to leave her with the prisoner? Alone? In her kitchen? She thought for sure the guard stayed as well. She'd even made up the guest room with the guest sheets, even though he wasn't exactly a guest. Company was company after all. Still, was this safe?

The prisoner had not moved. Charlotte peeked to be sure. Still slouched in the kitchen, inside the allowed square. Still staring at his shoes, apparently. He looked harmless enough, Charlotte supposed, even if he was a criminal.

"Well then," the guard offered after Charlotte was silent for a moment. He cocked his head slightly as he looked at her. She felt like the look suggested she was perhaps a little feeble. She couldn't seem to respond, though. "Guess I'll be going."

He rolled casually toward the front door, Charlotte's fingers sliding from their loosening grip on his arm as he moved. He let himself out and she just watched him go. She blinked a few times, taking it all in.

"Well, please have a pleasant day," she mumbled after he had already gone. She glanced around the room aimlessly.

Catching sight of the prisoner in the kitchen, she started. She rushed to the front door and locked it. This had taken up too much of her day already. So much remained to be done before Ward arrived home from work, prisoner or no prisoner, guard or no guard.

Charlotte quickly fetched the broom and dustpan from the kitchen closet, keeping an eye on the prisoner as she went. He was still a prisoner, after all, regardless of how harmless he looked. Then she swept from the foyer into the dining room, and then on into the kitchen. Doubtless the men had attempted to wipe their feet, but they were men. Surely they tracked something onto her floors. Really, she needed to mop as well. That would have to wait for the prisoner's square to be removed, though. There just wasn't much point mopping until that was gone.

She kept looking at the prisoner as she swept. He did not move, but Charlotte could not forget his presence. Could not concentrate on her work while worrying about him.

Well, she would have to do the work waiting in the other rooms of the house, she decided. Just until she learned to ignore him. She swept into the dustpan and emptied it before replacing the broom and dustpan in the kitchen closet. Laundry. That was just the thing. She'd get the laundry started. By the time that was finished she thought she'd surely have got a hold of herself.

She hurried out of the kitchen after taking one last look at the prisoner. Then she marched through the dining room to the hallway at the back of the house which led to the basement. She flipped the basement light switch and pulled the door shut behind her, to have a little privacy now that she wasn't alone in the house.

As she walked down the wood stairs, painted a thick gray, Charlotte noticed how prison-like the basement seemed. It seemed strange that she'd never thought of it before. The whitewashed cinder-block walls. The smooth, dark cement floor. The small, solitary room. It was a bit cell-like when she thought about it.

She snorted. There was work to do and she was still thinking about that silly prisoner. Well, that was enough of that. Straightening her posture, she marched over to the laundry machines.

In a large plastic sink next to the laundry machines, Ward's whites soaked in plain water. They'd been soaking from the night before. Charlotte always soaked whites in bleach water first, diluted of course so as not to burn holes. Then she rinsed before soaking them again in just water. The process was time-consuming, but it had to be done. Whites dulled far too quickly with just laundering alone, and actual bleach in the wash or even merely rinsed out whites could leave light spots on her nice colors. No, her multi-soak method was the only way.

She drained the sink of water and wrung out the excess, just in case any bleach remained. Then she loaded the whites into the washing machine, set the machine to hot, and started the cycle. After water filled the machine, Charlotte added the detergent. She always waited until the machine filled so the detergent would mix with water before sticking to the clothes.

The washing machine, of course, had been empty. The dryer as well. She never left the wash in overnight, either in the washing machine or in the dryer. Leaving wash overnight caused wrinkles or mold. No, laundry went from start to finish within a day or not at all.

She closed the lid to the washing machine to let it do its work. The hamper with the clothes still to be washed waited next to the machine. She always brought clothes down to this hamper when dirty, never leaving a pile on the bedroom floor. They had to wait, though, until the washing machine finished and the whites moved to the dryer.

Well that was it for the laundry. Charlotte had no more reason to loiter in the basement, avoiding the prisoner. She figured she might as well go and get used to having him around while she did her work.

As she closed the basement door and drifted back into the dining room, Charlotte realized she had not yet had lunch. The prisoner's arrival completely ruined her schedule. Otherwise, she would have lunched at least an hour before in order to ensure she would be hungry again when it was time to serve Ward dinner. She clicked her tongue and shook her head, deciding she better get it over with and salvage what she could have the situation.

The prisoner looked up at her when she entered the kitchen, but just for a moment. Before Charlotte could react, he stared downward again. In fact, she couldn't be sure she'd seen him move at all. She noticed he still stood in the same spot in the square. Apparently she really didn't have to worry about what he might do if not watched. This really was as safe as she'd been assured it would be.

Nodding quickly to no one, she set about making a small lunch. She was hungry, but lunch had to be small because it was so late in the day already. Otherwise, her stomach would not be empty again in time for dinner.

A sandwich was just the thing, small and quick. Wonder Bread, mayonnaise, leftover turkey, and sliced cheddar. Just like that. She didn't even have to scrub the counters afterward because she worked on a square of waxed paper. She poured a wholesome glass of milk and it was all done.

Turning around to take the sandwich to the kitchen table, she saw the prisoner. She realized she had been so focused on preparing the sandwich that she'd forgotten about him. He was just so easily forgotten.

Looking at the little man, Charlotte paused while holding the glass of milk and the plate with the sandwich. The guard said that someone would be by every morning to feed the prisoner. Surely, though, that could not be all the poor man was allowed to eat? It seemed so cruel.

Well, the state could run their prisons as they liked and she could treat people in her home how she liked. Charlotte marched up and held the plate and glass out to the little man. "Here," she said. "I imagined you might enjoy a little lunch."

He didn't look up. Charlotte stood for a moment, holding out the sandwich and milk, waiting to be thanked. Finally, she set the plate and glass in the square with him, figuring he must be shy from being ordered around for so long.

"I'll just leave this for you," Charlotte reassured the little man. "You can eat it when you are hungry."

She turned around then and repeated her efforts. Wonder Bread, mayonnaise, leftover turkey, sliced cheddar, and milk. Finally, she sat down at the kitchen table and efficiently enjoyed her lunch. She faced away from him, of course, so he would not feel self-conscious about eating. Surely his table manners were a little lacking and would prove to embarrass him.

When she finished, though, she saw that the prisoner had not touched the sandwich or the milk. Not a bit. In fact, he had pushed the plate and glass just outside the square, as if the unaccustomed kindness contaminated his imaginary cell. He shuffled as she stared at him.

Charlotte huffed. He did not have to eat if he really was such a stickler for the rules, but she did not have to put up with ingratitude.

She wrapped up the sandwich in the waxed paper she had used for preparation and placed it in the refrigerator. That would be lunch for the next day. The milk she just drank, though she did not want it and it made her a bit nauseated to drink a second glass. There was just no way to wrap milk up to save. Then, she washed the dishes and glasses, dried them, and put them back in the hutch.

She hoped the prisoner paid attention to all the work she had to do, which she had to do because of him. He had to notice, even if he would just stare down, if she checked. They were in the same room after all.

"Well," she told him as she turned to look. As she expected, he did not look at her. "I simply do not have time to worry about you. I have to start my husband's dinner." The prisoner did not respond and Charlotte huffed again. Then she turned and retrieved her Dutch oven from the cabinet.

Dinner was roast again. A good roast required a few hours to cook, but it was hearty. That was the sort of thing Ward needed to stay on top at work.

She told Ward once, just thinking out loud, that cooking roast all the time was a little repetitive. He told her that she could cook anything as far as he was concerned, take a Chinese course and cook *chop suey*. She shook her head, remembering. That was Ward all over. He did not even stop to recall that Chinese dishes gave him those late night heartburns. No, roast was repetitive, but it was reliable.

Charlotte set the Dutch over on the kitchen counter and preheated the oven. Then she got the roast from where it defrosted in the refrigerator and unwrapped it from the white butcher paper. Setting it in the Dutch oven, she rubbed the roast with garlic salt and pepper and onion powder. Even rosemary for flavor, as always. Then she washed potatoes from the decorative potato box in the corner and carrots and onions from the crisper and sliced them over the roast. By the time the oven was ready, Charlotte was finished. She set the lid on the Dutch oven and placed it inside the oven.

Wiping her hands together as if they were dirty, which of course, they were not, Charlotte looked around the kitchen. Dinner was started. It would be ready just when Ward arrived home from work. One more task accomplished.

She happened to glance the little man's way again. He looked so pitiful, Charlotte thought, all meek and crestfallen as he was. So wretched. Surely he was sorry for whatever crime he committed. He certainly looked sorry to her.

"Now see here," Charlotte insisted, marching over carrying one of the kitchen table chairs. "I understand that you are a prisoner and are accustomed to following prison rules. However, you are staying within my home now. This is the situation and we have to live with it." She paused, waiting to see if he would react in some way. He did not.

"My home is not a prison and I will not have it treated like one," Charlotte pronounced, standing very straight. "We are civilized people in this house and we act accordingly."

She jammed the kitchen chair into the square. The little man flinched.

"While you reside in my home you will act civilized as well. If you are tired, sit down. Use the washroom when you need to. As long as you do not misbehave, and be sure to stand in your appointed place when the guard arrives in the morning, then we do not have to live under lock and key."

She smiled, not that the little man would know since he was not looking at her and all. No matter, Charlotte felt she made her point. Besides, she had the next laundry cycle to attend to.

Turning away from him, Charlotte marched through the dining room and down into the basement. This time she did not shut the door behind her, just so he would know she was keeping an eye on him. Quickly, she moved the whites to the dryer and put the next load in the washer. Then she started both machines and marched right back up into the kitchen, expecting to find him sitting obediently in the chair she had provided.

He was not, though. Charlotte gasped. The chair was pushed outside the square and the prisoner stood just as before. He had pushed her chair away from his area, just like the sandwich. Like it did not belong there and had to be removed.

"Now see here," she shouted at him, realizing with a shudder that she probably sounded like a guard. "If I offer you a place to sit, I expect you to be grateful. By all means, do not sit if you do not want to sit, but do not throw my hospitality back in my face. No matter how much you pretend, that square is not a prison cell. It is my kitchen floor. You are a guest and you will behave as such. Do you understand?"

The little man did not answer. He fidgeted as if he was trying really hard to pretend she was not speaking to him, but he did not speak in turn.

"I asked you a question," Charlotte demanded. "Be courteous and answer me."

The prisoner fidgeted more. "Ma'am," he finally whispered, hoarse like he was not used to talking anymore. "Prisoners are not allowed to have visitors without prior written approval. If visitors have been approved, then a visitation may take place, but only on Sundays."

Charlotte grabbed the prisoner by his orange coverall suit and yanked him out of the square. His eyes shot wide in apparent alarm.

"Visitations? So, I am a visitor in my own home? That is the last straw," she shouted, yanking him through the dining room. "Get out of my house."

Charlotte tore open the front door and flung the prisoner out onto the lawn. Then she quickly slammed the door shut again and drew the bolt. For a few minutes, she fumed in silence.

After a time, though, Charlotte's anger slowly was replaced by a growing panic. What had she done? She evicted a prisoner that the state ordered her to keep. What would they do to Ward and her? What would the neighbors think? Slowly, she opened the front door, just a crack, and peeked out.

The door flew inward, forcing Charlotte back, and the prisoner leaped onto her. His claw-like hands furiously grabbed at her throat and squeezed with a surprising strength. Charlotte gasped in shock, but she could draw no air.

The prisoner's eyes burned, blasting hatred full bore into Charlotte's own from only inches away. He pushed her backward with unexpected intensity, back through the foyer, back through the dining room, until he slammed her against the solid dining room table. The dishes, already placed for dinner, clattered from the force of the jolt.

Charlotte's throat gagged, futilely attempting to breathe. A black ring formed around the edges of her vision and her legs buckled. She sank to the floor, the prisoner's twitching hands squeezing ever harder.

And then, it stopped. Charlotte gulped feverishly at the air she could finally pull into her lungs and looked around wildly from where she was sprawled on the ground. The prisoner was no longer above her. She struggled to her feet, grabbing onto the dining room table frantically.

Then she finally caught sight of the prisoner again. He was back in the kitchen. Back in his little square, staring at his shoes as meekly and quietly as he had before. As much of a mouse as ever, harmless. Charlotte slid down onto the floor, still clinging to the table, and just breathed.

HOME IMPROVEMENT

I think it was a Tuesday when my house left me. Gone when I got back from the updated SEC filing requirements seminar in Akron. There I was, fresh home from the hustle and bustle of the city, only my home wasn't there.

At least, I'm pretty sure it was a Tuesday. All the big changes happen on Tuesdays. So, being a Tuesday, I shouldn't have been too surprised when I got out of the taxi and my house wasn't there, certainly not after Akron.

I was, though. I was surprised. For a second, I thought the taxi driver had dropped me at the wrong place, a vacant lot, not my home. I turned back around by reflex before I'd had a chance to think, to say something. He'd already driven on, though, off to do more carefree driving, the lucky dog. No need to worry about anything. Man, what a life.

When I turned again, as the situation sunk in, I saw that it was my home after all. Or, rather, it should have been. My house was just gone.

And when I say gone, I mean gone. There wasn't a piece left, not a shingle or a board. Even the foundation was missing, the yard too. There was just a hole.

It seemed like there would've been something that used to run in or out of the house, gas lines or power cables, pipes or coax wires. It was a blank slate, though. The hole was as bare as a de-linted navel.

Looking at it all, or rather at the nothing since the *all* was gone, I heard my neighbor Ralph come tromping over.

"Phil," he grunted, "what happened to your house?"

"It's gone, Ralph," I informed him. Ralph and I were always having these stimulating conversations because we were neighbors. Or we had been, before my house was gone.

"Can't believe I didn't see that."

I nodded.

"So was there an explosion or something? Gas leak?"

"No, Ralph, my house just left."

"Left? More like somebody stole it. You should call the cops."

But I knew better. Involving authorities would only embitter the situation, turn things rancorous. Did I even have a legal right to force her to return? After all, how could anyone have stolen my entire house? The idea was absurd. They would have surely left traces, paint chips or nails. There would have been giant horrible tracks in the mud from heavy diesel machines necessary for such a task, but there was none of that. No, my house left of her own accord.

"I'll handle it," I explained. "Police don't like to get involved in domestic situations."

"So what're you gonna do?"

"Get an apartment, I guess."

At that, Ralph tromped back over to his yard and continued raking. Or, maybe he hadn't been raking before popping over for our little chat. Maybe he spontaneously started afterward.

I hadn't really been upset before that moment. I definitely hadn't been angry. Suddenly, though, I desperately wanted to kill Ralph. It suddenly seemed possible that my house left me for him.

After all, when he trimmed his hedge, the one that ran along my yard, didn't he stroll over and do my side as well? Didn't he sometimes keep going and snow blow my front walk after doing his own? In being, or pretending to be, neighborly, he'd paid an awful lot of attention to my house. Maybe something had been going on, flirting. Maybe my house wanted more of that.

But then I didn't want to kill my neighbor anymore. Maybe I never had. After all, even if it was true, it didn't change anything. Leaving me for Ralph and just plain leaving weren't any different. Either way, my house still wasn't there. Meanwhile, Ralph kept raking.

So what could I do?

I got that apartment.

Hey, maybe I did move a little quick. So what? I couldn't just stand in the mud forever. I had to stay some place. It was a good apartment, too, the top floor of a turn-of-the-century house, big diamond windows and angled walls from the pitch of the roof. It looked like an urban version of a white barn. This nutty old Czech woman who lived on the lower floor and watched infomercials all day owned it. She never bought anything, but she loved to watch and tell people what garbage they were hocking. She was a fun one.

"It's not so big," she told me when she showed me around, "but that way you don't have to clean as much. Won't have to throw money away on OxyClean."

"I don't need much," I agreed. "I just want a place to sleep and relax."

The Czech woman *tsked* when I told her I lost my house. Her scraggly red-dyed hair shook. "Such a terrible thing. Work so hard for something and they take it all for one bad little patch."

I nodded, but only so I'd get the apartment. I didn't want to explain. She already suddenly wanted a credit check and a pretty serious deposit, best not to rock the boat more.

At the office, I mainly surfed the Internet. Ever since they'd found out my house left, most of my coworkers didn't come close. That even included my boss. I guess it was awkward.

"Hi, Phillip," Marge chirped brightly, leaning into my cubicle. A number of the other middle-aged office hens, all of whom had some strange fascination with coworker lives, clustered behind her, looking concerned. "How are you doing?"

"Fine," I replied, not even bothering to minimize the personals I was scrolling through. They'd be too timid to say anything anyway.

"Well, good," she said after a moment, apparently baffled that I hadn't suddenly opened my soul in response to her inane little inquiry. "That's good to hear," she pointlessly continued before she and the others withdrew to their usual spot on the other side of a nearby cubicle to loudly whisper about me.

That's about the most anybody had said to me in a while. They popped by to show their concern and then scurried away just as quick. Because of that, no one gave me any work to do for a while and no one noticed whether I really did anything. As you can imagine, I hadn't done much.

I don't even know why I was reading the personals. I guess I'd already browsed through everything else worth looking at with my sudden leisure time windfall. Regardless, one suddenly caught my attention.

Young Starter Home Seeks Driven Go-Getter.

Hey, baby, looking for a gal you can really sink your teeth into? I'm looking for a real *owner, someone who isn't afraid to get his hands* dirty. *I might be a little high maintenance, but I'll make it worth your while. Interested? Write me and we'll see whether you're up to the* challenge *or not.*

The house pictured was mine.

The hen cluster was still whispering around the corner.

So that was the story. It wasn't like I shouldn't have seen it coming. I admitted I had not taken care of my house like I should have, never paid the appropriate attention. Sure, I mowed the grass when I needed to. Well, once in a while. At least, I did when the city sent me demand notices.

I never edged, though. I never did any of the little things showing I was really interested, that I took pride. The eaves never got painted even though the white flaked off and the wood started to rot. All sorts of undone chores seemed neglectful in hindsight, all of a sudden.

The house let herself go as well. Plumbing leaked. The air conditioner didn't cool correctly. I suppose she felt there was no point if I wasn't that concerned.

Really, the surprise wasn't that my house was looking for someone else. It was that she hadn't done it sooner.

Sitting there looking at the ad, I realized I was actually happy that she was out on the market. I'd never been up to the work, changing furnace filters, paying mortgages, wrapping pipes so they didn't freeze, all that. It had been too much, the effort I had to spend to make things work with my house and me. All that responsibility on me. Frankly, it had been suffocating.

But suddenly I was free. Even though all the work I'd put in was wasted, at least I didn't have to do any more of it. It was never going to work, no matter what. At least moving on cut our losses without losing further.

It was awkward when I eventually went to see an attorney.

"Let me get this straight," the balding little old guy said to me, sitting in his musty downtown office. "You want to sell just the lot and not the house? The house isn't part of this?"

"That's right. The house is gone."

He took off his glasses. "Gone? Where'd it go? Shouldn't you try to get it back before selling? You'd get a whole lot more."

"I'd prefer to just sell the lot," I insisted, and kept on insisting, through all his questioning about insurance policies and such, until he finally gave in and sold the lot for me.

Mind you, he looked at me funny even then.

Personally, I thought it was only fair. She'd never asked me to pay the mortgage or alimony or anything. She still had all the furniture, but it seemed like that all was part of her anyway. It didn't seem right to try to take it.

It was quite a long time before I saw her again, years even. Believe me, I wasn't looking. I was just out for a walk in a pleasant upscale neighborhood, affluent and charming beyond my means, down near the river. Suddenly, there she was. Sitting on a double-sized corner lot.

I almost didn't recognize her. She must have done pretty well for herself without me. When we were together she was just another subdivision starter home sort of place. White-painted wood siding and asphalt shingles, that sort of thing. Cookie-cutter, bland and cheap, just like every other house on the block. Somehow since she'd been on her own, though, she'd developed into a forty-room Tudor mansion with textured plaster and alpine-themed carvings on the eaves.

Frankly, it was only because I'd spent so many years with her that I knew she was my house. The transformation was so drastic, but I'd know her anywhere.

For a moment, I thought about going in. I thought I'd just say hello, but at the same time I wasn't the same person anymore, either. Surely I had changed and things were different. She looked really good. But I thought better of it while standing on the sidewalk. Really, I was still the same guy. I wasn't being truthful with myself if I thought things had changed. I didn't make a scene. Instead, I just kept right on walking.

It was all right. I'd done okay as well. I wasn't a Tudor mansion or anything, but I had a good sound system in that apartment and a very respectable collection of vinyl. I had nothing to worry over and didn't have to work nearly as much as before. Most of my time just rolled by pleasantly, with me frittering away the afternoons listening to velvet music.

Really, that's all I'd ever wanted. Now everybody's happy.

A BRIEF ACCOUNT OF THE GREAT
TOILET PAPER WAR OF 2012

I. Introduction

In the interests of ensuring that future generations will have an accurate understanding of the Great Toilet Paper War of 2012, I, Winston Feldman, have taken it upon myself to record this document containing the pertinent facts. History is interpreted through the lens of the party who relates the story, and as my wife is the more sociable of our little pair, I thought it best to preemptively correct any exaggerations and omissions that she may make. I only wish the matter to be clear.

The basic facts are simple and straightforward. The parties to this dispute were my wife (Eva) and myself. The core of the dispute? Toilet paper.

II. Origins of the Conflict

My wife and I, it should be clarified at the outset, have different views on the subject of maintaining a home. I prefer a well-ordered situation where chores are unambiguously delineated and promptly performed. My wife, on the other hand, prefers allowing our home to gradually decay into an advanced state of decrepitude while she passively witnesses such as if it were television coverage of some third world country. Obviously, this difference has been the cause of a small amount of marital strife.

The dishwasher is a perfect example. Like civilized people, my wife and I have agreed that she will empty the dishwasher and I will fill it, scraping the dishes first. However, my wife does not seem to be of the opinion that the proper time to empty a dishwasher is when it is full of clean dishes. Her view defines *time to empty the dishwasher* as when she has both the free time and the inclination, as well as not feeling the compulsion to do something else instead.

The frequency of such a conjunction of events generally means that the sink is constantly full of dirty dishes waiting for me to be able to wash them.

Toilet paper bears a certain similarity to the dishwasher.

Now, my wife and I aren't ridiculous people who would do something as insane as divide up toilet paper related chores. That would be absurd. If we did, I'm fairly certain that she would advocate similar procedures to the dishwasher and I would get the *short end of the stick*.

No, my wife and I are reasonable people for the most part. At least, my wife is when she isn't having fun at my expense *which she sometimes does*. Toilet paper is a simple matter of the person who uses the last of it being assigned the task of placing a new roll on the holder. That is simultaneously fair, reasonable, and logical.

However, I noticed that my wife was having a certain amount of difficulty with the arrangement. In brief, I kept finding empty toilet paper roll tubes on the holder. I could be certain that the guilty party in these cases was my wife, as in each instance I had not yet had cause to use the toilet paper.

Clearly, my wife simply overlooked this simple task. Believing that this oversight could be reasoned with, I reminded her of the importance of replacing the toilet paper.

I do not believe that she took me seriously.

Her reaction varied from reminder to reminder, though I was always careful to be calm and polite in delivering them. Sometimes she rolled her eyes. Other times she laughed as if I'd made some kind of joke. There were even times where she argued that the roll was not, in fact, empty. I might have been accused of being a word that rhymed with *banal*, but I wouldn't stoop *as my wife might have* to repeat such a thing here.

To be clear, a roll of toilet paper is not non-empty if there is but a single shred of tissue left that does not amount to a full, double-ply square. This is not disputable. Paper that is sometimes glued to the tube at the center of the roll as a result of manufacturing defects does not count, nor does ripped fragments. If a usable piece of toilet paper does not remain, the roll is empty.

I informed my wife of this well-accepted definition. She suggested that the empty roll itself might be used for wiping.

I still do not think she was taking me seriously.

Finally, my efforts in providing reminders began having some success. It was likely that she had become irritated at my frequent harping and merely wanted the noise to cease, as she may have stated, but the new rolls got on the holder. I think that counted.

However, the success was short-lived. I can understand the practice of simply setting a new roll on top of an old one if the old roll is close to being out but is not yet actually empty. This is a sane and efficient practice. It simply makes the new roll more accessible for when the eventual replacement occurs. But, my wife began utilizing this *setting* practice when the old roll was completely used. She even began using the new roll while it was placed in this unconventional manner. As one might imagine, I discussed this issue with her.

My wife insisted that she was merely trying to keep me happy. *Keep in mind, she was laughing when she said this.* She asserted that the demands on her time as an elementary school teacher were quite great and that she did not always have time to make sure the new roll was securely on the holder. I countered that though I seriously respected the demands on her time, *which may not have been strictly accurate*, the schedule requirements of a head procurement officer for a major direct marketing conglomerate were no less severe and that I still made time.

I believe my wife was unconvinced.

Compliance at this point was sporadic at best. Occasionally, my wife would place new rolls of toilet paper correctly on the holder. Sometimes she would merely set the new roll on the old. Sometimes she would even ignore replacement entirely. I still believed compliance was possible and regularly monitored the bathroom in order to issue appropriate reminders.

Of course, I replaced the toilet paper each and every time I used the last of the previous roll.

III. The Conflict Escalates

In retrospect, it might have been a bad policy decision to begin haranguing Eva to replace the toilet paper roll whenever she forgot. I realize that this may have seemed a trifle more authoritarian than was appropriate for relations between a man and wife. Eva may have said something to this effect, but that is neither here nor there.

However, at the time, this seemed like an appropriate way of dealing with the situation. My wife would not expend enough attention to remember to change the toilet paper. In response, I made it something she could not ignore. Simply, I did not shut up until the roll was changed. The rationale was that it would be unpleasant enough that she would remember the next time.

Unfortunately, I believe this tactic pushed my wife over the edge.

It was about that time that I believe my wife began deliberately replacing toilet paper rolls improperly as opposed to merely overlooking proper toilet paper replacement. The *setting* method became her standard. I even think she attempted to beat me to the end of the toilet paper so she could have the opportunity for improper placement. If pressed to fix this when not watched properly, she would actually install the roll backward so that it unrolled from underneath instead of from over the top.

I increased the volume of my reminders.

No longer content to simply replace toilet paper rolls improperly, my wife actually began removing full rolls I had placed properly and setting them on top of the holder. When confronted, she laughed and claimed I was being paranoid. However, careful tracking of incoming toilet paper, outgoing empty rolls, and replacement rates proved that I was correct. Also, there was the fact that she occasionally performed her malfeasance while I was using the bathroom. That example was pretty difficult to refute.

Clearly, this was a declaration of war.

Now, I pride myself on being a patient, rational man, *Eva's claims to the contrary notwithstanding.* I attempted reason far longer than any other man would have. Well after it was undeniable that polite negotiations would have no effect, I kept trying. Only after all other avenues were utterly exhausted did I resort to aggression.

I glued the toilet paper on the roll.

That's right. I glued the toilet paper on the roll. I unwound each roll, applied glue to the underlying surface of the respective paper, re-rolled, and then let the glue set. Then I placed the glued roll on the holder. I did that to each and every roll in the house.

The idea was ingenious, in my humble opinion. Quite simply, the roll could never be empty. It couldn't be unrolled for use, therefore paper would always be available. My wife would never have to worry about replacing toilet paper again. I, of course, carried my own, usable supply around with me.

This solution did not improve the situation.

IV. The Conflict Escalates Further

I suppose it should come as no surprise that, since we had not resolved the conflict within our home, it spilled out into the larger world. It is unfortunate, given that innocent bystanders were caught up in the middle of our hostilities, but this was war. War recognizes no boundary lines.

My wife began removing toilet paper rolls from holders in the bathrooms of our friends and family. Most of the time, she practiced this toilet paper terrorism when she believed I would shortly use the restroom. But sometimes, in attempting to be proactive, she engaged in skirmishes that I ended up having no part in. I mean, sometimes I just didn't need to use the bathroom, though she had no way of predicting that.

Homes of friends throwing dinner parties, her parent's condo in Florida, every bathroom at my place of employment, no water closet was off limits to her guerilla tactics. No one was safe. There was more than one civilian casualty.

Sometimes she just performed her *setting* trick. Those cases will be referred to as the polite incidents. Others were more brutal, such as when she unrolled entire rolls and wound it around the respective bathroom. A few times she just flushed it all down the toilet, one flush at a time.

War is hell.

Of course, I was not completely blameless in these extra-territorial actions either. Too many times to count were the toilet paper holders in mock bathrooms at hardware superstores and such appropriately stocked with actual paper. Sometimes the filling was permanent, as in the glue actions described above. When the superstores carried toilet paper, I used that. When they did not, I brought my own. Regardless, my wife was treated to the sight of properly filled toilet paper roll holders wherever she went, whenever possible.

V. Ultimate Force

Of course, it was evident that this situation could not continue. The theater of war had spread too far. The rules of engagement had become too encompassing, too ill-defined. There had been too many civilian casualties.

For example, my dear aging great aunt Ethel was forced to sit in her bathroom for hours, desperately and fruitlessly calling for assistance, during the barbeque celebrating her eighty-seventh birthday because my wife had preemptively stolen all the toilet paper. Unfortunately, we were all outside on the patio by the charcoal grill and did not hear her cries. And, contrary to my wife's assertions that I overreacted, I think it was more than reasonable to respond by having a semi-trailer loaded with Charmin delivered to her mother's charity gala. But, unlike my wife, I will be fair and allow history to judge our actions instead of attempting to bias the reader.

Regardless, there were getting to be too many places where we were no longer welcome, if not downright barred from under penalty of criminal trespass.

The time had come for ultimate force. Even in war, there are certain activities that parties to a conflict simply do not engage in. They are just too heinous, too extreme, too devastating. Even when threatened, no nation immediately responds with ultimate force.

However, despite all this there comes a time when the final force must be considered. A nation cannot be blamed for resorting to such an action in response to ultimate force itself, certainly. Moreover, it may also be resorted to when the costs of continuing conventional warfare would be too great. It can never be a light choice, but sometimes it is a choice that must be made.

Finally, I had no other option. I had to drop the bomb; I left the toilet seat up.

I admit this was not just a one-time occurrence. I am referring to systematic and regular leaving up of the toilet seat. I left it up each and every time I went to the bathroom. I went in and put it up when I hadn't even used the bathroom. I even snuck around in the middle of the night to leave the seat up when my wife wouldn't be expecting it. After all, this was ultimate force.

May God have mercy on my soul.

At this, my wife responded. It wasn't just a game anymore; this was serious. I had finally reached her. She dragged me into the den and forced me to sit down for a disarmament conference.

The den really was a smart choice, *and I still steadfastly maintain that the den was my idea, suggested while she was dragging me, and that she was not already dragging me there anyway.* Sure, we had decorated the room in a minor fashion, but neither of us ever used it for anything. The den was neutral territory. It was the sort of place for enemies to meet and be able to de-escalate while still saving face.

For her part, my wife agreed to attempt to remember to put new rolls of toilet paper on the holders. She also agreed not to misplace rolls merely out of spite or humor. In exchange, the toilet seat would be left down, and I would not berate her when she forgot. Of course, all extra-territorial activities were ended.

Really, it was about the best we both could have hoped for. The disagreement was not really resolved, but we had peace. Admittedly, it was a fragile peace, but it was peace.

VI. Détente/Conclusion

Though our differences were never actually settled, my wife and I have managed to carve out a livable state of mutual mild mistrust. No one had surrendered, but there were no more active battles. We simply have been unable to afford to continue the war, either of us. Even my wife had to admit that.

Sometimes my wife does forget proper toilet paper placement. Often, I let it go in the interests of marital harmony. But, if it becomes too frequent I begin forgetting the toilet seat again. She recovers quickly. Of course, she has often threatened to resort to toilet paper malfeasance as a reminder if I am ever the one to forget, though that would seem to run contrary to her frequent accusation that I never forget anything.

The household situation is somewhat tense, always, but my wife and I manage to get by. This is just the way our world is. Our home is a Berlin divided, with us the bound yet separated peacetime soldiers staring warily at each other from our respective trenches.

Such is the history of the Great Toilet Paper War of 2012, *and anything my wife says to the contrary is an outright lie.*

THE BRICKLAYER'S AMBIGUOUS MORALITY

A shriek erupted out of a beat-up amplifier, dusty with cigarette ash, on the day Derek was killed. Derek, a bony kid with rat-fur brown hair and a ripped decal-covered bass on a thick leather strap undulated closer to and farther from the old amp, warbling the feedback whine. He grinned toothily, swaying in place in the crowded bedroom. Stiff, dark bath towels were wadded up in the sills to block the windows.

"Bust," a deep voice boomed from the other side of the bedroom door, causing Derek to jump, startling him from his reverb fascination. He stared as the door throbbed with the pounding of a fist.

"Bust," the voice yelled again as the door flew open, flung by the thick arm of a solidly built tall kid in an old black Camel shirt with the sleeves ripped off. His longish dark hair, the sides shaved to the sun-colored scalp, swished erratically as he barreled into the room. A blue-painted brick went with him, clutched in his hand.

Derek rolled his eyes. "Larry. . ."

"Bust. Bust. Bust." Larry closed the door behind him and threw himself onto the unmade bed amidst wads of already worn clothes. He curled his large fingers behind his head and leaned back into a pile of pillows, yawning. "Bust's over."

Derek looked at Larry like he wanted to be sure that Larry was finished. Larry looked calmly back, perhaps indicating that the act was indeed complete.

"Dude," Derek finally spoke. "You've got to cut that out. What if I'd flushed my shit?"

"There's no pisser in here, Derek. No way to flush." Larry yawned again, bored, and rested the blue brick on his chest. Then he stretched out, the back of his head on his palms.

41

Derek looked around at the piles of crumpled McDonald's bags, precariously stacked CD cases, and dirty laundry. Like maybe he might have forgotten a toilet somewhere in all the junk. "Well, maybe I would have eaten it or something. You still wouldn't be able to mooch any."

Larry grunted. The blue brick jumped a small amount on his chest from the sudden breath.

Noticing, Derek said, "What's with the masonry?"

Larry grabbed the brick and whipped his arm like he was going to toss it up above his face and catch it, but pulled his arm back without letting go. He set it back on his chest. "It's my rifle."

Derek waited, plucking lightly at the strings of the bass. "Okay."

"Really. It's some retarded ROTC thing. I carry it around all the time and act like it's my rifle. Supposed to teach me responsibility or something." He sat up on the bed, sliding the brick down to his crotch.

Derek strummed faster, beginning an actual song. "You wouldn't have to do shit like that if you went to gym, like everybody else," he yelled over the music. "No more wearing gay green uniforms all over school. No more other stupid shit."

Larry tossed the brick and caught it, for real this time, though not above his face. "It's no dumber than gym, not unless you're one of the assholes who's enlisting and thinks it counts for something there. Besides, in ROTC they don't make you hang out with a bunch of naked guys."

Derek looked up from the bass. "What? Are you bitching about showering again?"

Larry pushed a pair of half-folded jeans off the bed with a boot-covered foot so he could stretch out a leg. "So? It's gay, dude. I'm not doing it."

"Man, nobody likes it. They just man up and get it over with. It's better than marching around playing war."

"Whatever," Larry muttered, pretending to sight the brick in on Derek. "You just want to see my junk."

Derek, concentrating, didn't respond. He played instead. His thin fingers plucked and smashed furiously at the thick strings. Notes spat out of the dirty amplifier like orange welding sparks. He hunched over, entranced.

Larry sat on the bed, apparently not impressed. He looked around the room aimlessly, maybe trying to find something worth looking at. If so, he didn't seem to find it.

"There," Derek snapped upright, thrusting the bass outward in a stylized metal concert *finishing move.* "Check that shit out."

"What?"

"What? That was Iron Maiden's *Phantom of the Opera.* I nailed it."

"So?"

"So? Dude, it's like the hardest fucking song there is. And that was without a pick. Just fingers."

Larry laughed, his belly rolling. "Chill out, I'm just messing with you. Yeah, you can play. We know this."

Derek sighed, relaxing back into his former slouch. "That's not cool, dude. Don't mess with Maiden. It's just not something you do." He shifted the strap so the bass rode lower.

"What?" Larry laughed again. "You going to go all rock psycho on me with your guitar? Smack my shit up? I got a rifle, man," Larry said, brandishing the brick. "Nobody tells this soldier what to do."

"Cool it, Larry." Derek strummed the bass aimlessly. "Just quit fucking around about serious stuff like that."

Larry jumped up and stood on the bed. "Fucking around? Man, I'm on maneuvers." He held the brick out in front of him, lengthwise with both hands like it was even long enough to feel like a rifle. He leaped off the bed at Derek. "I'm engaging the enemy. It doesn't get more serious than that."

"Dude." Derek backed away, holding out his arms and letting the bass dangle.

"Present arms." Larry tilted the brick up. "Order arms." He pointed the brick forward again.

"Quit it."

"Fix bayonets, maggot." Larry stabbed at Derek with the brick. "Gut 'em like dogs."

"Cut it out," Derek screamed right as an explosion shook the small room.

The two boys stared wide-eyed at each other. Then their eyes trained to a wisp of smoke trailing off the end of the brick. A spot of blood spread out from the center of Derek's dirty white Ozzy T-shirt.

Derek slumped to the ground, his eyes still wide. Glassy. Larry gaped at the brick and then at Derek. His mouth moved silently. The brick slid out of his hand, inexplicably crashing into three equally sized pieces as it hit the carpeted floor.

~*~

Larry chewed on the end of a pencil, scratching at his now fully shaved head, the center of his scalp glaring whiter than the sides like a landing strip. He hunched over a test preparation course book on an uncluttered desk, at the same time apparently trying to keep his square shoulders upright in a blue oxford shirt new enough that the fold lines from the package still showed. Underlining a passage in the prep book, he frowned and the skin on top of his head wrinkled. A heading at the top of the book's page read *ASVAB Study. Chapter Three.*

"B," Larry muttered to himself. He held his place in the book with a fat finger and flipped to an answer section in the back. "Fuck!" He pounded a ham of a fist down onto the desk. Then he flipped back to the page held by his finger and traced his way through a paragraph.

The desk stood next to a muted blue wall marred by faded rectangles shaped like sloppily hung posters. A few shreds of scotch tape clung around the faded spots. Across a brown shag-carpeted floor, scarred with recent vacuum cleaner marks, an immaculately made bed was the only other furniture in the room.

Larry continued to read, his lips moving noiselessly. He bent closer to the book, staring hard. His hand motioned to run through hair on his head that wasn't there. He looked up at his hand, startled to have caught himself, and then returned to reading.

"Laurence?" an older man's baritone voice questioned through a closed door to the room, though with a slight clipped note of command, followed by a series of light knocks.

Larry's eyes darted up and he jumped out of his unpainted metal folding chair. He breathed quickly. Then he marched over and opened the door.

"Sir," he said, standing up straighter and then pausing, "Mr. Rinn."

A plump balding man in a sweater-vest, considerably shorter than Larry, strode into the room past him, one leg staying stiffer than the other, resulting in a bit of a limp. Mr. Rinn's hands were shoved deep into his pants pockets, bulging the pleats. His eyes took in the room, though he didn't look at Larry until after he ambled over to the bed and sat down heavily, his knees catching slightly. The rigidly tucked blanket pulled up from the mattress.

"Been straightening up a bit?" Mr. Rinn pulled his hands out of his pockets and placed them on his knees, giving a military air to his bearing. "Doesn't look much like I would have expected. Nothing like Derek's room."

"Yes sir," Larry responded, looking down at the floor. "It seemed like it needed it."

Mr. Rinn took a sharp, deep breath. "Cut the *sir* shit, Laurence. I work for a living. Call me Bill like you always do. Now, sit down, for Christ's sake. Close that door too."

Larry jumped to shut the door like it was something he was embarrassed to have forgotten. Then he turned the folding chair around at the desk and sat down facing Mr. Rinn. He crossed his arms across his chest and then uncrossed them. Finally, he gripped the kneecaps of his squarely bent knees tightly like he needed to make sure his hands stopped wandering.

Mr. Rinn watched the little performance. He shook his bald head and sighed. "Your dad's been worried about you, Laurence. Even got up the guts to give me a call about it." He paused to look at Larry. "I guess I can see why."

Larry managed a weak smile. "I'm fine. Just trying to stop screwing around all the time. Got to do something someday, right? I guessed it was time," Larry babbled nervously. His voice trailed off as Mr. Rinn stared at him.

"So your dad says you're trying to enlist and won't let him talk you out of it." Mr. Rinn rubbed his unevenly shaved chin. "That you're asking to go to Afghanistan. Maybe even Iraq."

"That's right, sir." Larry looked down at the floor.

Mr. Rinn nodded slowly and then looked around the room again slowly, as if scanning a perimeter. He looked at the blank desk and walls. He looked at a small, framed picture of Derek hanging by the bed, a black ribbon draped over one corner. Finally, he looked at Larry's shaved, unevenly tanned, head.

"Laurence," Mr. Rinn said slowly. "What happened to my boy, that wasn't you."

Larry stared at his boots.

"It wasn't your fault. Maybe you want it to be, maybe you don't, but you think it is. Maybe I even wanted it to be, just to explain things. But it's not."

Larry swallowed. "I shot him."

Mr. Rinn leaned forward, glaring. "With. . . a. . . brick."

Larry kept looking at his boots, like if he sat there long enough then Mr. Rinn would get up and leave.

Mr. Rinn folded his hands and rested his chin on them, still staring at Larry. "It was a brick, not a gun. You couldn't have known what would happen. No one could. It doesn't make any sense. It was just something that happened."

"But it wouldn't have happened," Larry's head snapped up as he screamed, his eyes streaked red and pulsating with stinging wetness, "if I'd acted like I was supposed to."

"And?" Mr. Rinn scoffed. "My son would be here if you hadn't pretended a brick was a real gun just in case it somehow went off? Just so some freak thing wouldn't happen?"

Larry looked away again. He wiped at his eyes with a thick hand.

"What about the idiots who told you to do it?" Mr. Rinn asked. "Is your teacher responsible? How about the factory that made the brick?"

"They all did what they were supposed to," Larry responded quietly, looking at his boots again. "I was the one screwing around."

"And?" Mr. Rinn stood up off the bed. He paced around slowly in front of Larry. "You're going to run off and join the army then? Be a man?"

Larry scowled, but his head stayed down.

Mr. Rinn puffed out his chest and stopped in front of Larry. He looked at him as if he was waiting for Larry to speak. Larry stayed quiet.

"Maybe you won't hear what I'm telling you," Mr. Rinn muttered, his chest deflating. "Maybe I'm wasting my time, but I've been there. I didn't have a choice."

Larry glanced up, timidly. His hunched shoulders twisted slightly with the movement.

"The only thing I had to depend on was the guys with me." Mr. Rinn paused, his eyes drifting like he was looking further than the walls of the room. Then they came back. "I just hope nobody has to depend on some kid using the army to try to fix his life. Those kids have too much on them already. It isn't right to make things worse."

Larry and Mr. Rinn stayed silent for a couple minutes after that. Then, without speaking again, Mr. Rinn left. Larry watched him go as he pulled the door shut behind him.

Finally, sitting up straight and taking a breath, Larry snapped himself out of it. Without standing, he turned the chair around to face the desk again and pulled in. He picked up his pencil and flipped through the book. As he read, he started twisting the pencil between his fingers. He twisted faster and then faster still. His hand clenched hard, trembling, and the pencil broke in half.

Suddenly, Larry screamed, his arm snapping to backhandedly fling the ASVAB book off the desk. It crashed into the wall and then, instead of falling, it floated lazily around in the air. A few loose papers, carried with the book, fluttered lightly around it, orbiting peacefully. Eyes wide, Larry stared.

CHANGES FOR THE CHÂTEAU

Christien listened, pressing his ear to the door of the American's room. He could hear the buffoon showering, but he knew that much already. That's why he had come. Inserting the passkey into the old lock as quietly as it would go, he glanced a dignified look down the hall to be sure no other guests were about.

Of course, there would be nothing amiss about Christien entering a room. He was the manager of this rural southern French hotel. His tasteful, albeit faded, somewhat dusty dark blue suit suggested confidence and promised respectful service. Workmen's clothes like his brother Jean's would be suspicious. A nice suit, however, inspired trust.

He turned the key and then stopped. There was no way the old lock would open quietly. It was merely better to move quickly and hope the American would not hear. The unchanging sound from the shower indicated that he had not.

Truly, Jean would have been more suited to this particular task, even if his clothes were not the best for unnoticed entry. Once inside, they would be more appropriate, fit for scrabbling around under tables and such, bending and stooping and whatnot. Jean was, after all, the repairman. Their mother had handed down their respective roles, and the attire that went with them, back when she ran the hotel. Christien and Jean would never have thought of altering such an established arrangement after her death in the nineties.

However, Christien was aware as he delicately pressed the door open that Jean did not have the finesse for entering rooms. There had been quite a few beatings before Christien and Jean finally reached this conclusion.

The heavy oak door did not creak as it slowly pivoted open. Christien made sure Jean kept the tarnished brass hinges well-oiled for precisely that reason, but one could never be certain with hinges that old. The hinges simply had their tempers, as all old things did.

Christien slipped quickly into the room. He did not close the door all the way so that he could not open it again in an instant, instead leaving it open just a crack so noise from the hall would not alert the showering buffoon. The passkey had also been left on the outside of the door in the lock.

Pausing to make certain that the showering continued unabated, Christien glanced around the room. The American's tawdry, blue nylon roller bags on the bed seemed particularly tasteless against the background of the deep burgundy duvet that had once belonged to Christien's mother, but one had to accept such an event when running a private hotel. Still, Christien bristled at the idea, even after so many years.

He collected himself, smoothing his lapels. Regardless of his personal feelings, the loutish idiot was a guest. Christien had a task to perform.

The door to the shower, closed, was located on the other side of the room across the bed. Christien tiptoed over to the door, opened it, and entered the bathroom.

Inside, the sound of the shower was considerably louder. The American, luckily invisible behind the mustard-yellow linen shower curtain, splashed and sang some horrid song about a *loco-motion*.

The linen curtain and the bare metal rod bolted crudely into the aged plaster walls were relatively new additions. It had not been necessary before so many Americans came to the hotel. Civilized people could use a shower without making a mess, but Americans seemed to get water everywhere.

As the shower splashing continued, Christien found the water valves behind the sink. His errand would have been simpler if the hotel possessed a central boiler room, but it had not been designed with considerations of this particular procedure. Looking toward the shower, Christien cut the hot water.

The shower erupted in high-pitched screams. Or, rather, the American in the shower erupted in high-pitched screams. The shower was likely uninvolved in the matter. Suddenly, the linen curtain flew open.

"You."

The dolt was wearing a hat. Christen could not grasp this, a hat in the shower, but it was not a shower cap. Instead, it was a baseball hat, blue with a large red C on the front. A hat? In the shower? What would be next?

"What the hell are you doing?" the hatted lout demanded.

One hand still on the valve, Christien gave a polite wave with the other. Then, as the flabby, pasty American charged out of the shower after him, Christien fled the bathroom.

Running for the hallway door, Christien looked back and noted that the American had managed to wrap a towel around his midsection. Apparently he possessed some decorum though Christien could not be sure why it surfaced under those particular conditions. And though that was the purpose of towels, Christien did not relish the image of the hotel's towels touching the naked idiot.

Reaching the hall door with time to spare, Christien slipped out and shut it behind himself. He locked the door with the passkey, which he promptly pocketed. Predictably, he heard the imbecile run into the door a moment later. Christien turned and hurried briskly away down the hall.

~*~

Christien had not been particularly concerned for his safety. There was an element of risk involved in sneaking into a guest's room in that manner, but it was merely part of running the hotel. He knew he would reach the door before the clumsy fool. He certainly had enough practice to be sure. It was likely that he spent more time on such foolishness than on any other aspect of running the hotel.

Of course, he had not always had quite so much experience at annoying guests. Events had not always been so unproblematic. There were incidents, some even necessitating visits to the local doctor, particularly when he and Jean first decided on their unusual hospitality practice.

He recalled one young American couple specifically. He remembered that the husband was an attorney back in the United States because a certain amount of litigation had been threatened after the episode.

Christien crept into their room as they slept, perhaps exhausted from their trans-Atlantic flight. He was nervous, standing there with the antique soup tureen and his grandmother's ladle. Jean had conceived of the plan, but only Christien was sufficiently fed up with their mounting losses to carry it into effect. Still, standing over the sleeping couple, he hesitated.

He steeled his nerve by examining their impact on the room of his hotel. Le Château D'Espoir stood some distance outside of Orange, so there were few artificial lights outside, but the moon shining in the window revealed enough. Their cheap clothes were all over, not unpacked neatly, as any other human being would have done, putting them into the provided walnut armoire. There were even damp underpants hanging from the lampshade. The indignation that filled him was more than enough to clang the silver ladle loudly against the sterling soup tureen.

"*AAHHHH!*" the couple screamed in unison, shooting up from bed.

"Good evening *Monsieur* and Madame," Christien bellowed, banging the ladle on the tureen again. "It is the middle of the night. How are you sleeping? Is the bed quite comfortable? Perhaps you would like me to open the window?"

Christien thought politeness would improve upon the idea of an impromptu alarm. He wanted to ensure that the couple would wake up fully and become so confused that further sleep would be impossible. This *hot and cold treatment* struck Christien as the ideal formula.

"I could even provide you with a restaurant recommendation though I must advise you that all the restaurants will be closed. It is, after all, quite late."

"What in God's name are you doing in here?" the husband cried. The wife, apparently quite terrified, hid beneath the blankets. "What's the meaning of all this?"

Christien, when he imagined how all of this would go, thought that the man would jump out of bed to attack at such a moment. Indeed, the husband did just that. Christien pictured how he would dash for the door and the husband would become entangled in the blankets, allowing Christien to escape unharmed.

Unfortunately, for some reason, Christien panicked at that moment and darted right instead of left, which took him around the bed toward the bathroom, instead of toward the safety of the hallway. The husband did get caught in the blankets as expected, but he recovered and chased around the bed after Christien. Christien was trapped.

"Why are you in our room?" the husband demanded.

Christien barely knew what he was doing. Suddenly, he leaped upon the bed and ran right over the frightened wife.

"Please, *Monsieur*. You selected the economy rate for your room. I must do this."

When he reached the edge of the bed, he dropped to the floor. He planned to run for the door, but the husband had jumped onto the bed as well, running thoughtlessly across his own wife, in order to follow. There was no time for the hallway door, so Christien ran around the bed again.

"Picking economy means you break in here in the middle of the night and scare the hell out of us?"

"Yes, *Monsieur*. Americans all want bargains or luxury, but all our rooms are somewhat similar. My brother and I, what could we do? We had nothing to call a *suite*, so we made economy and deluxe the same, only the economy comes with annoyance."

Christien and the husband made several more circuits around the bed as this repartee went on. The husband came no closer to catching Christien, and Christien came no closer to escaping. Also, the wife took no steps to avoid further trampling. The chase simply continued.

"Then change us to deluxe and get the hell out of our room."

"I apologize, *Monsieur*, but that is not possible," Christien pleaded. "My brother and I realized that the deluxe rate conferred no benefit if economy guests could simply change. I must continue to annoy you."

"But you didn't tell us any of this when we checked in," the husband protested. "We didn't know. We never wouldn't have taken this room if we'd known."

"Precisely, *Monsieur*. It would not have been an annoyance if you had not been surprised. Warnings are not included in the economy rate. That would constitute a *frill* and would violate the spirit of *economy*."

Christien was becoming alarmed. All the explaining and running wore him out. The American husband turned out to be in much better condition than Christien had anticipated. Christien couldn't evade him much longer.

Luckily, the wife finally acted. She threw the bedside lamp at Christien, hanging damp underwear and all. Her aim was poor, though, and she struck her husband instead.

Christien decided that the mistake was not all that inappropriate. Had not her husband trampled her as well? Surely he deserved striking just as much as Christien.

Regardless, the husband fell, and Christien managed to escape through the hallway door. Of course, there was a scene at the front desk later. Jean and Christien's plan still had a few problems to be worked out at that point.

~*~

The operation of the plan became smoother over time. Christien and Jean discovered how to handle the tantrums and avoid the assaults. Well, mainly Christien discovered this. Jean never managed the annoyances very well, but their mother had made Christien swear to watch out for his brother, so Christien handled everything.

Though they learned to make it work, events did not turn out quite as expected. An unforeseen happening had occurred, a frog in the butter if you will.

Christien and Jean were at the front desk when yet another American came in. He was very clearly a businessman attempting to resemble a motorcycle hoodlum. He wore a leather coat and bandana, but the coat was quite expensive and made to appear tattered, and the bandana still had creases from being starched.

"Welcome to Le Château D'Espoir. Would *Monsieur* care for a room?" Christien asked.

Of course, Christien was the one to address the potential guest. Jean was present, but he performed repairs, not greeted guest. Only Christien dressed professionally and spoke. Jean had just been at the desk to go over a list of materials that Christien needed to order in the next month.

"Sure would." The *biker* put his hands on his hips. "I'll take one of the *economy* rates."

Christien started. Even Jean looked concerned, and Jean was not one for noticing when he should be alarmed.

"*Monsieur* is *aware* of our economy rate?"

"Guy in my office stayed here last summer and told me all about it. I just had to check it out."

Christien stiffened. "Certainly. Would *Monsieur* care for a southern or northern facing room?"

The odd man shrugged. "Doesn't matter. I just hope I don't get any *surprises* while I'm here." He winked at Christien.

He winked. The cretin actually winked, trying to be subtle about not being subtle. The vulgarity of the gesture sickened Christien.

But what could he do? The entire concept of the economy rate entailed rooms plus annoyances. However, if the guests wanted them, for whatever reason, could the annoyances even be considered annoyances? Christien suspected that they could not. The whole idea that he and Jean had worked so hard on would fall apart.

So, he charged the American double. Not just double, but double the price of the deluxe. That was the only solution Christien could think of quickly.

Soon, Americans arrived all the time asking for the *economy* rate. Word apparently traveled and they wanted to experience Le Château D'Espoir's economy rate *treatment*. Triple the price for economy became the hotel standard. It simply became a service that Christien and Jean provided.

Strangely, the idiots were hostile during the annoyances, as if they were actually annoyed, but then they laughed about them later. As long as Christien safely escaped the rooms at the time, there were no aggressive consequences.

Frankly, Christien and Jean were baffled. These incomprehensible Americans took the meticulously considered scheme and turned it completely around. The hotel was a joke, but Christien and Jean were obligated to continue the farce if the hotel was to stay in business. In other words, they had no choice.

Of course, this mode of life was not without problems for Christien and Jean. It could be trying at times, and sometimes it just became too much. This morning was just such a time for Christien.

An elderly American couple wandered into the hotel, wanting directions to a small restaurant nearby. As usual, Christien was at the desk. Perfectly polite, he directed them.

"Yes, *Monsieur* and *Madame,* it is quite simple. Proceed West on United States highway one-thirty. After about a mile, make a U-turn. It will be on the right."

"Huh?" the old man scratched his head. "Highway one-thirty? What is this? We're not in the states. We want to go to the little place on the other side of town, the one with the blue-striped awnings. Where are you trying to send us?"

"I am simply directing you." Christien smiled. "You wish to go to the Denny's. It is just down the highway, but you must make a U-turn as you cannot turn across a highway."

"Denny's?" the withered woman protested. "We're in France."

"No, we are not," Christien screamed suddenly, his face turning red, pounding both fists upon the desk. "We are in New Jersey and I am directing you to the Denny's."

The older American couple left quickly without asking further questions. It was all right; they were not guests anyhow. They had simply stopped in to find their way. If they had been guests, Christien should have made certain that they were there for the economy rate before reacting like that.

But sometimes he could not help himself. There was only one way for Christien to stomach what he and Jean had done to their mother's hotel in order to keep the Americans' business. Quite simply, he imagined that it was not his mother's hotel anymore.

In his mind, Christien pretended he was the proud proprietor of the Econo Lodge in Bordentown, New Jersey.

FORM OVER SUBSTANCE ≈ EGGS OVER EASY

"Frankly, I wouldn't buy a dollar from you for fifty cents." Donald leaned confidently back in his tall leather chair in his walnut-paneled corner office, crossing his arms behind his head. Financial tomes, which Donald never used but thought lent an imposing atmosphere to the office, lined shelves on the walls by the hundreds.

The kid squirmed in the square-edged orange cloth-padded chair centered in front of Donald's ornately carved oak desk. Still leaning back in the chair, Donald looked down his Roman-ish nose condescendingly at him. "In sales, you've got to walk in like you know all the answers and your guy just has to listen up to make good. You're trying to sell me *you* right now, but I don't think even you'd buy yourself."

The kid shakily reached up and pulled his tie knot so he could swallow. Donald saw the shaking and could tell the kid saw him see it. "I. . . I'd be an excellent addition to Pellin Billing Services, Mr. Vandernacht," the kid stammered. "I was just curious how clients saved money by outsourcing billing and payment."

Donald humphed. "I'm supposed to make you worth something? No good." He shook his distinguishably balding and graying head. "I need men who are useful to me, not the other way around. See yourself out."

"Thank you for the opportunity," the kid blurted as he bolted away from Donald, cowering at the same time, toward the thick wooden door on the other side of the office.

Sitting his chair upright again, Donald crushed the kid's resume and tossed it expertly into his polished chrome bin. Another useless sheep, another college grad with good grades who didn't think he had to fight to convince people to give him a chance. They all were like that, no self-starters.

What he needed, Donald thought, was a few more of himself. He had never crawled, never needed someone to babysit him once he went to work. He'd had what it took, been his own man. The chest of his dark suit jacket puffed out as he remembered.

At dinner, one of Donald's father's cronies had gone on and on about how his billing and payment service was going to make a fortune because businesses would pay anything to dump their worries on someone else. The old man hadn't been talking to Donald, but Donald knew his chance when he saw it. A week later, Donald was in the old man's office with a whole stack of willing clients. He hadn't been sure how the service worked, but he knew his dentist and his doctor and he got them thinking they needed what the old man had. He figured the details would come later. It had been a gamble, sure, but it paid off. None of the boys from his neighborhood had his kind of success. They were all still slaving for someone else, complaining how they never got any breaks.

"Poor dear, didn't work out?" Ms. Rott asked offhand, her sensible black heels tapping the stone tile floor as she efficiently clipped her way to Donald's desk, her gray hair coiled in a bun so tight that it stayed motionless as she walked.

Donald frowned, but not at her. "Not a bit. He was just a boy, didn't know how to do anything. Probably would have even had to hold his hand in the men's room."

"Well, here is the next gentleman's resume," she stated plainly, setting the paper in front of Donald on his desk so the text properly faced him for immediate reading. Her eyes darted around Donald's desktop, probably looking for the kid's resume to remove, but stopped immediately when she saw it wasn't there.

Ms. Rott was a gem. He'd found her working in a lawyer client's office. The lawyer said she was a perfect worker. Donald pounced when the lawyer retired, hiring Ms. Rott before she could even walk out of the old office door. Since then, she took care of everything from reception to filing. The billing service itself was automated so Ms. Rott was all he needed, other than salesmen to get more clients. It was almost as if she was born to perform her work. And yet, she always credited Donald with running a tight ship. She acted as if she really believed the office operated flawlessly merely because Donald was at the helm.

Honestly, her rigid faith made Ms. Rott far more valuable than her impressive efficiency. He never felt a flicker of doubt when puffing up for a potential client. After all, as long as Ms. Rott believed Donald could do what he said, it made it a little bit true. Because Ms. Rott didn't doubt, the potential client never doubted either. Soon, the potential client was a pleased, current client. Then Donald just found a way to make the bluff real. That faith was a money factory.

"How's he look?" Donald bantered, pretending to read the resume.

Ms. Rott paused, which was unusual, so Donald glanced up at her. He kept his head down and only moved his eyes so she would think he was amused and didn't need the information. However, this signaled something serious. Knowing whatever it was might save him some possibly embarrassing mistake. Yet another reason she was indispensable. "Yes?" Donald prodded.

"Well, he's a clown, Mr. Vandernacht." Ms. Roth pursed her lips in obvious disapproval. "I don't see what he thinks he's doing here. He has no business applying for a position with this office, not dressed like that certainly."

Donald chuckled. It was probably just another wet-behind-the-ears-kid borrowing his dad's suit. Donald could always tell. Those kids weren't businessmen and didn't have a clue how ridiculous they looked. No doubt this interview wouldn't be any better than the last. Still, Ms. Rott seemed to measure everyone against Donald. He didn't expect quite that much.

"Now, Ms. Rott," Donald playfully chided, "let's not doom the boy before he even gets in here. After all, we're professionals, even if he might not be. We can afford to be courteous enough to let each argue their case. Nothing beyond that, though. They have to step up to the plate for themselves."

Ms. Rott stiffened. "I'm sure you know what you are doing, but I mean—"

"Please show the boy in, Ms. Rott," Donald cut her off. He was careful not to let show how much he deferred to her. Better to treat her as an entertaining distraction. Anything else might damage that golden faith.

"Of course, Mr. Vandernacht. I'll send in the clown."

She turned precisely and clipped out of Donald's office. He chuckled again. The old girl appeared to be feeling her oats. She didn't usually crack jokes though Donald found he didn't mind it as long as she only did it when they were alone. Donald looked down at the resume. He wasn't going to read it and spoil his first impression, but it would be good to at least find out the poor kid's name. Giving the appearance that his decisions were not solidly founded wouldn't do at all.

JoJo Warbentinkle. Donald flinched. He read the name again; to be sure he hadn't misread it. There was no mistake, though. The paper clearly read *JoJo Warbentinkle*. Donald shook his head. No one could help what his parents named them, or what his last name was, but surely any man who could cut the mustard would change a name like that. A man's got to know how to be taken seriously.

JoJo Warbentinkle. What a ridiculous name. Donald started to laugh, but he stopped abruptly. There was a clown standing in his office doorway.

The clown wasn't the figure-of-speech sort of clown. It wasn't someone who dressed foolishly and didn't know it or a showboat who played an idiot to amuse friends. No. Standing in Donald's office doorway was an authentic, cotton-candy-and-big-top-elephants sort of clown. The resume slipped through Donald's fingers onto his marble-topped oak desk.

"Good afternoon, ladies and germs," the clown greeted him, taking an exaggerated bow. His red conical hat, white puffball on top with white dots down the front, fell from his head as he bent over. With a snap of his white-gloved hand he pretended to fumble, only tapping the hat and causing it to spin in midair instead of catching it. With another snap, he *accidentally* knocked the hat right back onto his head.

The outfit didn't stop at gloves and a funny hat either. He had boat-sized white shoes with red laces and a baggy red one-piece suit with white puffballs running down the front. His face was even painted white with some sort of thick greasepaint, complete with red smudges around the lips, eyes, nose, and cheeks. Donald noted those things one by one as he stared. Finally, the clown grinned and did a jazz-hands *ta-da* gesture.

Donald snapped to. Staring conveyed an impression of bafflement, a sense that the person staring was at a loss as to how to proceed. That was unacceptable. "Of course. Come in, sit down. By all means." Donald motioned at the cloth-padded chair in front of his desk, inviting the clown in out of a loss for any other way to react.

The clown paraded across the room with high strides, each footstep squeaking like a dog toy. When he arrived at the chair, he dropped to all fours and circled quickly like a cat stalking a mouse. After giving the seat an exaggerated sniff, the clown hopped onto the chair. He crossed one leg over the other, at the knee, and assumed an overly dignified expression.

Donald was sure this was a prank. Some joker wanted to see him flounder when a clown walked in for a job interview. It was too ludicrous to be real; it had to be a joke. Someone wanted to make him look like a fool. However no one jumped out to spring the surprise and laugh. There wasn't a camera in his office, at least as far as he could see, or anyone hiding behind his furniture. Surely something like that would be necessary. The best part of a prank is the look on the victim's face. Who would play one and not be around to see it? Who would play this kind of prank anyway? Certainly not Ms. Rott and Donald had no other employees.

The more Donald thought, watching the clown stick his thumb in his mouth and blow out his cheeks as if they were balloons he was trying to inflate, the more Donald realized that the most probable explanation was that this man was a complete lunatic. Possibly even dangerous. There was no telling what this man might do if he dressed as a clown to go to a job interview. "So," Donald spoke slowly, avoiding eye contact by pretending to read the clown's resume, "Mr. Warbentinkle is it?"

"JoJo Warbentinkle," the clown replied, nodding slightly as if unaware of the unusual character of the name.

Donald nodded back, stalling. His mind reached frantically for something else to say. He could just throw the clown out without saying another word, but that would show frustration. That wouldn't do. It certainly wouldn't be what Ms. Rott expected of him, not after his speech about letting the clown plead his case.

"Of course," the clown patiently explained, "JoJo Warbentinkle isn't my real name."

"No?" Donald asked, following the clown's lead for the moment.

"Of course not. No one is called anything like that. That's exactly why I picked it as my clown name, for the pizazz."

Donald wrinkled his brow. "Why did you put your clown name on your resume?"

"Because it's who I am," the clown explained slowly, as if to a child. "I'm a clown. It's my life."

Donald nodded as if this reasoning were actually rational. Of course, it wasn't, but Donald thought it safer not to prompt any further explanation. That would probably just get even more bizarre. If pressed, perhaps the clown would even turn violent.

Clearing his throat, Donald shuffled the resume, even though it was a single page. The most prudent course seemed to be to treat this like any ordinary interview and act as if people always came for salesmen jobs dressed as clowns. Sure. Happened every day. Then the clown would simply leave when the interview was finished. Donald would just shake his hand and say something about keeping his resume on file.

"So," Donald continued, making sure to look at the resume and not the clown, "it says here that you attended the LeRue Academy. I'm not familiar with that particular institution. Is it a liberal arts school?"

"It's a clown college. Obviously," the clown jeered, not bothering to hide his apparent irritation. There even seemed to be a suggestion in his tone that Donald might, in fact, be an idiot.

Donald quickly moved on. "No matter. College is a big waste of time, in my opinion. A man has to have that piece of paper, but colleges don't teach anything useful. You're either born with what it takes or you're not."

The clown smiled, neither agreeing nor disagreeing.

"So," Donald said once more, "why don't you tell me about a time that you had to deal with someone who just wouldn't listen to reason? What did you do? Give me some feel for how you work."

"Okay." The clown sat forward, apparently excited to tell a story. "There was this show I was in near Poughkeepsie where I was supposed to build a tower out of these huge rainbow plastic blocks from a big pile. This other joker was building a tower of his own, but instead of taking blocks from the pile he kept taking my bottom block and crashing my tower. Every time I showed him the pile that he could use and rebuilt my tower, he'd just go and do the same thing again."

"I see," Donald remarked, trying not to signal that the chosen story was utterly absurd. "What did you do?"

"What did I do? I smacked him in the face with a wedding cake, of course. What do you think I did?" The clown sat back in the chair again, apparently quite satisfied.

Donald turned his head to the side and scratched his ear as if he had some sort of itch. He was afraid he couldn't keep his face straight any longer. When he managed to compose himself, he turned back. "That was certainly an interesting approach," Donald conceded, "but I don't see how that solved anything. You didn't get him to stop taking your blocks, did you?"

"Who cares?" The clown snorted, making a honking noise. "It was funny."

"Well," Donald replied, pausing for a moment, "that wasn't really what I had in mind. Let's try something else, shall we?"

"I'm game if you are, thin-pants," the clown said with seeming eagerness. He sat forward again, elbows cocked and his hands on his kneecaps.

Donald leaned forward as well, resting his elbows and his arms on the marble top of his dark oak desk. "Let's say you've taken a potential client out to lunch, but he tells you he doesn't need anyone to do his billing. He thinks he can do it fine on his own, always has. What would you do?"

Without hesitating, the clown sprayed Donald in the face with seltzer from a spray bottle that just seemed to have miraculously been ready in his hand at precisely that moment. Donald forced himself not flinch, didn't even let himself sputter. Instead, he shut his eyes as the seltzer splashed over his face and poured down onto his desk, soaking the papers and files on the desktop. Donald waited until the spray stopped before wiping off his face with a sharp motion and opening his eyes. He glared at the clown. The seltzer bottle was mysteriously gone again.

"Mr. Warbentinkle," Donald said sternly.

"JoJo Warbentinkle," the clown countered. "You have to say all of it or none at all."

"Yes. Well," Donald growled. "I'm afraid that I don't think you are a suitable candidate for this position. I fail to see how clowning makes you a good fit for selling services to our clients."

"Oh, I see." The clown stood up angrily. His shoe squeaked sharply as he stomped his foot. "I can't have the job because I'm a clown?"

"Well—" Donald backpedaled, surprised by the clown's sudden aggression, "it's just that—"

"The fact that I'm a clown has nothing to do with my capability to perform this job." He slammed his fist down on the top of Donald's desk. This squeaked as well. "I am a clown. My father was a clown and his father was a clown. My father's grandfather may not have been a clown, but my grandfather's grandfather was a clown among clowns. It's bad enough that there isn't enough circus work and I have to lower myself to this, but I am proud to be a clown and I can do this job just as good as any of you non-funny people."

"I... I'm sure you can," Donald stammered. "I just think it's an inappropriate way for a salesman to behave. Surely you agree."

"Inappropriate." The clown looked like his face was turning an angry red, but Donald couldn't tell with all the face paint. "That's discrimination. We've got laws in this country about denying jobs because of lifestyle, thin-pants. I should sue."

"But—" Donald's brain raced. Was being a clown a lifestyle? Clowns couldn't sue for discrimination, could they? He couldn't be sure.

"You know what?" The clown snatched his resume off Donald's desk, soggy as it was, and wadded it up. He threw it at Donald as hard as he could. It was wadded into the shape of a chain of origami elephants. "I know all about jerks like you. I wouldn't work here if you begged me." The clown turned and stormed out of Donald's office, squeaking as he went.

After the shock wore off, Donald slowly got up from behind his desk and crept over to his office doorway. He peeked out and nearly ran into Ms. Rott.

"Well, he really was a clown, wasn't he?" she remarked.

Donald cleared his throat and straightened up. "Don't be ridiculous," he said in an overly deep voice before catching himself and switching to his normal tone. He adjusted his tie and the lapels of his dark suit coat. "He didn't make me laugh once."

LAST KNOWN SIGHTING OF THE HMS THOUSAND THREAD COUNT SHEETS

Lamar dreams himself in a lifeboat, caught in a sea storm in the middle of the Neiman Marcus menswear section. An elderly English butler in immaculately pressed evening dress hand feeds him *pâté* sculpted into the crowned heads of Europe while less fortunate shoppers and store clerks perish in waves capped by wet loafers and sport coats. Enrique, clad in a custom Vera Wang wedding dress, screeches from atop a jewelry counter for Lamar to risk everything to dive in and save him.

The sound of Joan Jett singing "I Hate Myself for Loving You" rips Lamar away from Neiman Marcus and flings him back into his dark bedroom, illuminated only by the flashing glow of Lamar's cellular phone sitting on the nightstand. Lamar reluctantly reaches his freshly manicured, light mocha-colored hand out from under the blue satin sheets. He clutches the phone, sighs from under the sheets, and pulls the phone to his ear.

"It's late, Enrique," Lamar mumbles. "What the hell do you want?"

"Oh, so you know it's me already?" Enrique's grating voice slurs from the phone speaker. "What, you screening your calls? Should I feel privileged you answered this time?"

Lamar sits up, casting off the sheets before clicking on the *chrome in motion* lamp sculpture on the ebony nightstand. He rubs his shaved and moisturized scalp with one hand.

"Of course not," he replies, attempting a soothing voice. "I set a special ringtone just for you. Just like you wanted."

"Oh? Is that so?" Enrique's slightly mollified voice asks. "What is it?"

"Uh. . ." Lamar stammers. "The 'Don't You Wish Your Girlfriend Was Hot Like Me' bit from 'Don't Cha.'"

Enrique snorts. "You know it." The sound of fingers snapping pops through the phone.

Lamar brushes imaginary lint from his waxed chest as he listens for Enrique to keep talking. "So. . ." he draws out slowly, "what do you want?"

"What do I want?" Enrique snaps back. "What do I want?"

"Yeah," Lamar sputters. "It's late, Enrique. I was asleep."

"Oh, I don't know," Enrique huffs. "Why would I call? Why would I want to talk to my man once in a while? That'd be crazy since he obviously doesn't miss me when I'm not around."

"Enrique, are you drunk?"

Enrique snorts again. "I better be or that wannabe Freddy Mercury bartender is being stingy with the tequila. What else am I going to do since you never want to be seen with me?"

"Enrique, don't make something out of nothing." Lamar reaches for the clock radio on the nightstand. "It's midnight and I'm giving a pitch presentation in the morning. That's all."

Pulling his hand sleepily back, Lamar accidentally knocks the clock radio off the nightstand. Reflexively, he lurches to grab it and drops the phone onto the bed in the process.

"Oh," Enrique's voice echoes into the bedroom out of the dropped phone, "slick boardroom man has swanky Madison Avenue GQ things to do. No time to waste playing with little Enrique-boys."

Lamar's slender fingers lightly touch the falling clock radio, but it slips through his grip. He winces, automatically anticipating the crash of plastic and metal against the dark hardwood of the meticulously polished floor.

"You think I'm not good enough for you except when you need some," Enrique's voice prattles on.

The clock radio meets the hardwood and the floor ripples and splashes like a violent coffee river. As if it was a cliff diver, the clock radio slides almost instantly through the undulating surface and disappears, making a *gluck* noise. Circles erupt and roll from the point of impact. They pitch and heave, like bubbling hot tar.

Lamar stares, eyes wide and arm still reaching. The floor continues to flex, bubble, but the motion begins to calm. Eventually, there is only a slight rise and fall, as if a body was breathing under a thin cloth.

"Lamar? Lamar?" Enrique's voice spits in irritation out of the abandoned phone. "Don't you be ignoring me."

And then the phone goes silent. The screen illuminates briefly, displaying a *call ended* message. Shortly after, the phone goes dark.

Lamar seems oblivious to the phone. He rubs his eyes and stares at the floor. The floor, however, does not move. Lamar scans left and right, but the hardwood boards appear normal.

"Must have still been partway asleep," Lamar mutters, chuckling. He sits back up in bed. His body reclines back until his head rests on the satin covered pillow. He takes a deep breath and closes his eyes.

A moment later, Lamar opens his eyes again. He purses his lips. Then he rolls over and leans off the side of the bed. Watching carefully, he swings his arm down at the floor. Instead of banging into the wood, his fingers pass right through. The surface of the floor ripples from the disturbance.

Lamar starts, jerking his hand back. "Huh," he mumbles, his eyes following the flow. As he watches, liquid wood quickly drips off his hand.

When the floor stills, Lamar again swings his arm. He splashes the floor around like the agitator on a washing machine. The floor swirls and eddies, though the grain of the dark wood is visible on the surface regardless of the movement. The floor slowly settles again.

"I wonder," he says quietly, reaching a cupped hand toward the floor. Gingerly, he scoops up some of the liquid and pulls it toward his face. He holds it close and watches the little puddle of wood. Then he takes a sip.

Pffffftttttt! He spits and coughs violently, fingers snapping to clutch the edge of the bed to keep himself from falling. His chest heaves and he clenches his teeth, nearly retching.

"Awful," he says repeatedly between spits. "Nasty." He wipes his mouth and looks mistrustfully at the floor though it's motionless.

Lamar looks at an elegant gold watch on the ebony nightstand. Grabbing the watch, he pulls one of the silk sheets off the bed, rolls it into a long rope, and ties the watch to one end. Then he dangles the watch off the bed, watching as the end of the sheet slips from view into the liquid of the floor.

More and more of the sheet disappears from sight as Lamar lets it slip further into the floor. He pulls it up a little and then lets it sink back a couple of times. Then he grabs the bed with his other hand and leans over far, letting the sheet go as far as he can by plunging in his arm to the elbow. He stirs his arm around in the lukewarm murkiness, trying to feel for a bottom.

Finally, he sits back up on the bed and reels the sheet back in. He feels it, but the sheet is not even damp. He sniffs the sheet a few times, holding it to his nose, but doesn't smell anything.

Then Lamar dips the watch end of the sheet into the floor again and makes his way to the end of the bed, dragging the sheet along in the liquid and rippling the surface as he goes. He drags the sheet from around the nightstand side of the bed to the foot and then to the other side before pulling the sheet back onto the bed and wadding it up.

He looks around the floor for a moment and then looks behind himself at the wall immediately behind the bed, suddenly remembering that it's there. Digging his heels into the mattress, he arches his back to place his palms on the wall and pushes. The bed, however, doesn't move.

"Great," Lamar murmurs, "but how's that going to help get me out of here?"

Gritting his teeth, he grabs onto the side of the bed hard and swings himself over, letting his lower half sink into the unseen depths. He kicks furiously, but he merely slides through the liquid as opposed to swimming. The floor appears unwilling to bear Lamar's weight.

His toned arms flexing, Lamar pulls himself out of the muck and back onto the bed. Breathing heavy from the exertion, he scratches his head. He tries patting his dark green silk boxer shorts. Completely dry.

Suddenly, the phone lights up and Joan Jett begins to sing again. Lamar snatches the phone and hits talk.

"Enrique. I–"

"That's right," Enrique's shrill voice shrieks from the phone. "I hung up on you. I hung up on Mister *I can't be bothered to go to one of Enrique's shows.*"

"Enrique, this isn't the time."

"Hey, you won't come down here then I'm going to shake it and see what happens. I'm sure somebody here would want to be seen with Enrique."

"I can't come down there," Lamar waves his hand wildly in emphasis even though it can't be seen through the phone. "I can't go anywhere. I need help–"

"Damn right you need help," Enrique prattles, interrupting again, "if you don't do something to keep this fine ass. I even bet some of these guys would want to get married."

"Enrique, that's not important. My floor–"

"So marriage isn't important? Or is it that Mister and Missus Brooks Brothers tight ass think the pink triangle is classy as long as it's not with some Puerto Rican gay-boy?"

"Enrique–"

"Get your butt down here, or I'll find me someone who will. I'll start trolling and see what's biting today," Enrique squeaks before hanging up.

"*Aaagghhhh!*" Lamar screams at the phone, holding it in front of his face. Then he drops the phone to the bed and holds his head in his hands.

As soon as he does, Joan Jett repeats her tired refrain.

"Enrique, I've got a real problem here," Lamar screams, snatching the phone up again. "Don't hang up."

"Oh, I'll hang up," Enrique chirps cattily. "I'll hang up and keep hanging up. Just don't think you'll be getting any of your pretty fairy beauty sleep if I don't see your ass at this club right now, 'cause I'll just call back. I'll do it, don't you think I won't. You might as well get down here, and hope that I'm not already with somebody by the time that you do."

"But–"

"You know I'll do it," Enrique snaps. "Don't play, you always lose."

"Enrique," Lamar yells into the phone, but the call is already disconnected.

A few seconds later, as Enrique promised, Joan Jett sings yet again. Holding the phone, Lamar looks and shakes his head. The same twenty seconds of "I Hate Myself for Loving You" plays over and over again.

Finally, Lamar reaches over and sets the ringing phone gently on the nightstand. Taking a deep breath, he throws himself over the other side of the bed into the curious liquid below. His body slides in with a small splash. And, in a few moments, the bubbling calms and the floor is still again.

MONKEY! MONKEY! MONKEY! MONKEY! MONKEY!

To be fair to Elaine, no one would reasonably expect to find a cymbal monkey upon opening the hood of an automobile. It isn't like any assertion is being made that Elaine is helpless with respect to cars, or that women are in general. This is not a story that deliberately attempts to perpetuate that sort of stereotype. No, this story believes that most men would have been just as baffled to find themselves in Elaine's situation. Though it is always possible that this story will be unintentionally sexist for other reasons, it is not attempting to intentionally be so by denigrating Elaine's mechanical competence.

Frankly, there were few things Elaine despised more than feeling helpless. It didn't come up particularly often for her, but it was something she feared.

One of Elaine's core obsessions in life was preparing for any incident that might come her way. She strived to be able to handle anything, literally anything. In fact, as an attorney specializing in guiding clients through the vagaries of business formation, it was her job. She took courses and attended improvement seminars. She sent away for practice models and home study kits. Anything she could do to familiarize herself with a potential problematic situation with respect to which she had been previously unfamiliar, she did.

Still, despite all of her preparation, Elaine's fear persisted. There just seemed to her to be so many ways one could be helpless, no matter what one did. She worked tirelessly, but despaired of ever filling all the knowledge gaps she might need to.

However, an automobile emergency was definitely something Elaine was prepared for. As her rental car continued to rev, though progressively less loudly as it slowly lost momentum on the rural highway near Donovan, Illinois, she was unworried. She expertly guided the 2012 Honda Accord over to the side of the road and put the car in park, leaving the key in the ignition. Then she popped the hood and stepped out to have a look.

That look was when Elaine encountered the cymbal monkey in the engine compartment.

Now, many people feel compelled to peek in the engine compartment of their cars after a breakdown despite having little reason to do so. Perhaps it is instinctual, even when people have no reason to suspect that they will have the slightest clue what they are looking at. Unless there is something obvious, like a cable popped off the battery with a sign labeled *must be connected for the car to run*, people without any automotive familiarity would be ill-equipped to remedy the respective fault no matter how long they looked. Still, they tended to look anyway.

And Elaine looked as well though she had a reasonable expectation that she would understand what she was looking at. She had taken several automotive courses at a local tech college. She'd studied car manuals and had performed routine minor maintenance on her own car, such as changing oil, rotating tires, and replacing alternators. Though her navy skirt suit was not ideal apparel for auto work, and though she would not have currently possessed parts or correct tools for most major repairs, Elaine felt confident in her ability to handle or at least diagnose many automotive problems. For more major issues, she was of course prepared with her cell phone and the number of the rental agency roadside service.

So, when she looked into the engine compartment and saw the cymbal playing monkey, Elaine felt validly and justifiably confused.

The odd little toy was just sitting in there, dressed in a little yellow shirt and red and white striped pants, banging away at its cymbals furiously. *Bang! Bang! Bang! Bang! Bang!* Its mouth was constricted in a pained, tooth-bearing, and jaw-clenching grin. Its eyes were wide and popped like those of an electrocution victim. Above all else, it banged its cymbals with no sign of stopping or winding down.

Being acquainted with the components of an automobile, Elaine noted the absence of an engine (along with the required pistons and such components), an alternator, and a battery. Also missing was a radiator, any place to insert oil, and less critical items such as a windshield wiper fluid reservoir. In fact, the cymbal monkey, being bolted to the frame and coupled to various assorted rainbow wires that ran all over and disappeared into various portions of the car's internals, was the only occupant of the compartment.

At that point, Elaine's brain began operating on two distinct levels. She definitely knew enough about cars to understand completely that the cymbal monkey should not have been present instead of an engine. Elaine was not an idiot. She knew that there was no way that such a thing was normal, or that a cymbal monkey should be able to power a car. All of this she knew. She was neither ignorant nor delusional.

However, at the same time, another level of her brain recognized that the cymbal monkey was, somehow, her current situation. However inexplicably, the car had been operating with only the cymbal monkey. Unless the engine had been present previously and had only been swapped out by magic mid-drive, the car had been functioning in this bizarre state. The toy was just what she had to deal with.

Not grasping how the cymbal monkey apparently worked with the car, she looked to see if anything did, in fact, look out of place. Burned or disconnected wires, broken shafts or belts, she scanned for anything that would be an evident mechanical problem in any machine, whether she understood this particular one or not. But, the cymbal monkey and all of its wires revealed nothing immediately apparent.

The cymbal monkey, throughout Elaine's inspection, merely continued on its cymbals. *Bang! Bang! Bang! Bang! Bang!*

Whatever was the problem, Elaine guessed, the monkey didn't seem to be it. It was still going strong even though the car would no longer move. Elaine briefly pondered whether or not the cymbal monkey functioning was itself a symptom. Perhaps it only banged the cymbals when motion could not correctly be transferred to the wheels. However, recognizing that she didn't possess enough information and would merely speculate endlessly in that line of thought, she retrieved her cell phone and dialed the road service number.

"Ever Ready Road Assistance," a chipper young male voice answered her call. "How can I be of service?"

"Yes," Elaine replied, "my rental car has broken down. I think I'm going to need a tow."

"I see," the polite voice responded, heavy with feigned concern. "What seems to be the problem?"

Elaine hesitated, recognizing a dilemma. Surely the cymbal monkey was impossible. She considered merely conveying that the car wouldn't go and letting the dispatched mechanic see the monkey firsthand.

However, the fact remained that this toy was somehow a functioning part of this particular vehicle. She was not familiar with such a machine, but someone obviously was. If she expected the dispatched mechanic to be able to solve her issue quickly and efficiently, as it would be his or her job to do, Elaine would need to provide the best information that she could. Otherwise, without understanding enough about the situation, the mechanic might arrive without the correct tools or parts.

"Well," Elaine paused, weighing her options, "the cymbal monkey is clapping away like mad, but the car just slowed to a stop and doesn't seem to be able to go anywhere. I can hear the banging, but no revving anymore."

There was a pause on the other end of the line. "The cymbal monkey?"

"Yes."

"As in one of those little mechanical things that claps cymbals together?"

"Yes," Elaine snapped. "I know it sounds crazy, but there's a little monkey in there instead of an engine. He has cymbals and he's banging them together."

"You're telling me your car has a monkey instead of an engine."

"Yes. Just listen."

Elaine dashed over to the engine compartment and held the phone close. The monkey obliged, or ignored her, and continued its activities in any event. The cymbals continued banging. *Bang! Bang! Bang! Bang! Bang!*

"See?" Elaine shouted into the phone before noticing the *call ended* indicator. The polite young man had hung up.

Elaine paused to breathe and calm herself before attempting to call again. She determined to be less informative the second time. As she was composing herself, though, a beat-up baby blue Chevy pickup truck approached slowly from down the deserted highway. It pulled over gently, but haphazardly, nearby. She could hear what sounded like Waylon Jennings emanating from within.

The truck sputtered off and the driver side door groaned open. A short, heavyset old man in torn overalls lurched out before slamming the door, hard. As he ambled over to her amiably, Elaine noted that he had a blue and white checked flannel shirt on under the overalls and his head was covered by a black baseball cap with *Sun Microsystems* emblazoned on the side. Elaine reflected that it must have been made before they were bought out by Oracle.

"Having some car trouble, little lady?" the hick asked.

Elaine straightened herself up rigidly and dusted off her navy suit jacket. "Indeed I am," she replied curtly. "Have a gander for yourself."

The old man smirked on one side of his mouth and strolled past her to look under the hood. He froze as he caught sight of the monkey. Slowly, the smirk faded. He looked at the monkey, then at Elaine, and then back at the monkey again.

Bang! Bang! Bang! Bang! Bang!

"What's this," he finally asked her, "one of them hybrid cars?"

Elaine pursed her lips sternly. "No," she snapped. "It is not *one of them hybrids*. That is a cymbal monkey. Hybrids combine gasoline engines with electric motors. They do not utilize mechanized children's toys from the fifties and sixties."

"Oh," the man remarked, pushing up his cap to scratch at the little amount of dark hair he had underneath, "I didn't know."

"I guessed as much."

"What is it then?"

"I have no idea," Elaine screamed. "I just opened the hood and there the moronic thing was. It just keeps banging those stupid cymbals and the car won't go anywhere."

"Oh."

"Oh? Oh?" Elaine slammed her fist down on the roof of the car. She collected herself, taking a deep breath. "Look, have you ever seen anything like this before?"

The elderly hick pushed the bill of his hat up and looked again at the monkey. "Well, no. I used to have one of them when I was a kid, but it wasn't attached to no car."

"And," Elaine proceeded, "have you ever even heard of one in connection with an automobile?"

"Well, no. I can't say that I have," the old man admitted.

"Great." Elaine threw up her hands. "I'm *so* thrilled that a knowledgeable man stopped to lend a hand to poor, helpless little me. Where would I be without you? Such a great help you've been."

The old man sagged a little, chastened, as Elaine continued her tirade. He politely waited for her to finish. Afterward, however, he seemed unsure what to say next. Both Elaine and the old man looked at each other, silent.

Finally, the old man rubbed his chin with one hand and regarded the monkey. He opened his mouth as if to say something, but then he closed it again. Then he looked at the monkey some more.

Suddenly, a bright flash lit up his dim eyes. He marched right up to the edge of the car and smacked the cymbal monkey across the back of its head. The car roared to life.

Elaine's jaw dropped. "What the—"

The old hick hitched up his pants, despite the fact they were overalls. "There's a lot of things I don't know," he grumped, "a whole lot of things. But, I still get some pretty good results out of giving machines a good *whack* when they misbehave." He shrugged. "Works wonders sometimes."

THE ELUSIVE QUALITIES OF ADVANCED OFFICE EQUIPMENT

"When's the fifteenth's EU filing going to be ready for me?" the blond clerk demanded, pushing a two-level filing cart covered in cattle-themed gear.

"Huh?" I started. I tried to remember her name, presuming I'd even heard it yet. I'd been trying to appear busy, not sure what exactly I was supposed to be doing at this new job, when she stampeded into my office, scattering the papers someone had left on my desk sometime during the two weeks since I started the job.

"There's a deadline on the fifteenth." Her eyes closed a bit as she smirked. "Are you handling it?"

I tried to think whether I knew what she was talking about, but her cart distracted me. She used it to carry files, but as I mentioned earlier, it was covered in cattle gear. Horns ornamented the front. Spurs jangled on the rear. A saddle rode on top, leaving little room for files up there though luckily the cart had that lower shelf.

People seemed to do that at this office. Themes. Western was just this clerk, but everyone did something. Each was equally individual and equally strange. I'd seen people decorate their cubicles with toys and pictures before, but this was something else.

The clerk hadn't stopped at her cart either. She wore a huge black cowboy hat and snakeskin boots. Her belt buckle, at least the size of a salad plate and shaped like Wyoming, was silver with bits of turquoise.

The duds made it hard to concentrate. I wanted to drawl when I spoke to her, or perhaps challenge her to a shootout at high noon. These people seemed to take their themes seriously, though. I bet flippancy would not go over well.

"No one told me I was handling anything." I cleared my throat. "Am I supposed to be?"

"It's got your name on the weekly report," she said with a smile that wasn't particularly friendly. "You have to monitor what you're listed for. It isn't my job to tell you."

She thrust out an overstuffed tri-folder, jammed with so many loose multi-colored papers that it rounded into a roll, like a giant inedible Ho Ho. It thumped with a slight mushy echo on my particleboard desk. Somehow the file didn't explode from the force of the drop, despite all the worn, fuzzy spots where the tri-folder had been handled and folded over and over again.

"I'll take care of it," I backpedaled. "Don't worry. But what am I supposed to do?"

"Hey," she shot back, literally shaping her fingers like guns and pointing, inexplicably not using the cap pistols on her belt, "I can't tell you that part, I'm not qualified. You do what you do and then I just file it. That's why you get the big bucks."

"Okay," I said, which was apparently some kind of signal she'd been waiting for because she immediately stampeded back out. I watched her go, strutting like she was a ranch hand with his thumbs in his pockets despite the fact she was using her hands to push her cart.

Looking down at the overstuffed paperboard file, I didn't feel like a spooked deer anymore. I'd just read through it and look for some clue to tell me what to do next. I hadn't gone to as good a school as some people in the office, but I'd graduated right at the top of my class. I could do it. It might take me some time to figure it out, and I might make a few mistakes, but they had to expect that if they weren't going to train me.

I opened up the file and spread the papers out over my desk, but instead of actually looking at any of it I found I was looking at the blank wall of my office. There was a banged-up table and some empty bookshelves, all leftovers from previous employees. The unending white of the drywall, pocked with holes from old removed nails, looked particularly bare, with just the couple of degree frames I'd put up. My undergrad one had a big, light-colored gouge in the wood that I hadn't yet fixed with touch-up stain. My grad school one was really the only decoration since I'd sprung for the deluxe model with the lithograph of some neat old building on the main campus to which I'd never been.

Shaking out of it, I tried to make myself read through the papers for more than thirty seconds at a stretch, but I kept spacing out. I could technically read the contents. Everything was in English, or at least had a translation attached, and the documents weren't that complex. However, actual reading proved to be a challenge.

Everything possibly related to the file seemed to be in there, so I guessed I was expected to figure things out from context. Original documents, various responses and memos, related filings that perhaps I needed to take into account, all that was present. Some of it was stapled, some not. Some was held together with various kinds of metal or colored plastic clips. A few documents were just grouped by a roughly folded corner. A bunch were just loose though obviously parts of larger documents. Notes and highlighting in various inks and different handwritings were everywhere.

Regardless, I couldn't grasp what I was supposed to do with it all. Just handing me the file wasn't enough. I could spend all day reading without getting anywhere if no one gave me any kind of direction. Surely they didn't just expect me to know.

I marched out of my office and down the thin hallway with the worn beige carpet to the boss man's office. Well, one of the boss men, the boss man listed on the file. There were a lot of boss men. Since this one must have put me down for this project, he'd just have to give me some idea what it was he wanted done.

"Ha. They can say anything they want," my boss man said. His door was open, but he was on the phone. His safari-themed office walls were lined with trophy heads. However, since actual killing of African animals was frowned upon, the heads were all constructed from carpet remnants and old clothes. He probably thought they gave the atmosphere of a big game hunter without risking nasty visits from PETA. Of course, it felt to me like he'd gone berserk on the Muppets. He was built too stick-like to convincingly pull off the big game hunter look anyway.

My boss man looked up at me standing in the doorway. His expression made me think he was considering adding a real head to his collection, so I backed away. "That doesn't mean we owe them anything," he continued.

I stood over by a communal document preparation table in the hall, trying not to act like I was listening to the call. I also tried not to look like I was aimlessly wasting time in the hallway while busy people stormed by. I probably should have gone back to my office and worked on something else, but I didn't know if he'd let me know when he was done or what else to work on. I could have ended up wandering back and forth all day trying to talk to him.

I artificially busied myself messing with the staplers on the table. There were three, a small stapler and two increasingly industrial looking ones. Having exhausted the staplers, I shuffled around some paper from a blank stack. Then I stapled it a couple of times. I even added a few clips from a brown metal caddy next to the stack of paper. I tossed it all in the blue recycle bin when I heard the phone slam down.

The boss man was turned to his computer, rapidly typing, when I walked in. For a moment, I wondered if he'd forgotten me looking in the door before. "Yes?" he asked without looking up.

"There's a deadline on the fifteenth for an EU filing," I explained, "and I'm down for it."

"Well then," the gaunt little guy said, trying to lick his lip quickly. Because his lips were so thin, it only looked like he was flopping his tongue around. "I guess you better get cracking. Ha."

I sat down in one of the lightly padded wooden chairs in front of his polished mahogany desk. "I am," I responded, "but I've never done one before. I was hoping you'd run me through it on a high level."

He tried to lean back casually, but the stiff newness of his *Bawana* outfit spoiled the effect. It was an expensive-looking getup, but it just seemed tailored for a thicker man, bulging out at odd spots as it did. It gave me the impression that he'd swiped his dad's clothes.

"Just give it a try." He shrugged. "Try to put something together and I'll take a look. It's easier to start from there than for me to explain everything."

I tried to focus on him, but my eyes kept wandering around his office. He had this sickly cactus on the corner of his desk however, that was supposed to fit in with his fake dead animal theme. It looked like a deflated lime green cucumber with limp hair; I wondered if he watered it enough.

There was this bunch of crayon drawings next to the cactus, probably from his kids, on paper torn out of safari-related coloring books. They were stacked in a neat pile so they looked like an inbox of drafts for him to review.

"That's just the thing," I insisted, "I don't know how to get started. I don't know what to put together."

"Look," he leaned in and grinned, but the grin seemed to stretch beyond his thin face, "you're making this way harder than it really is."

There didn't seem to be anything for me to say. I waited for him to keep going.

"Look," he said again, smacking his palm with a small fly-whisk, "start out by summarizing the original papers and then move on to the cited materials. After that, take things point by point and explain what matches up and what doesn't. List it all out, being sure to explain and analyze completely. Finally, figure out some sort of a conclusion and write it up." He leaned back in his tall leather chair underneath what appeared to be a macramé wildebeest head. "It's simple."

And, as I listened to him, it suddenly was. I didn't know why it had seemed so impossible before. A detailed map of how I'd attack the project formed in my head and I started thinking of all the different arguments I was going to write. I suddenly felt an urgent need to get out of his office so I could start before I lost anything.

"Right," I said quickly, "I think I've got it."

"Good man. Tally-ho." He laughed. Then he turned back to his email. I bolted back to my office.

But then, sitting at my computer just as I was about to type, I didn't have it anymore. Whatever filled me when I was talking to the boss man drained away. Gone. Sucked right out of me.

It suddenly dawned on me that he hadn't actually said anything. He just threw out a few general terms and ideas. Was the whole business just a giant scam? Maybe nobody could tell me what I was supposed to do because there was nothing to tell. Maybe it was a con that got passed down person-to-person, each participant validating the sham of the previous. But, some client would have had to catch on if it was all crap. Right?

Maybe it wasn't crap. Maybe I should have already learned whatever it was. I'd done well enough in school, but maybe I just tested well and never learned what I was really supposed to pick up.

I stared out my office window. I could see for miles since the office was so high up. Being that high made everything look flat and colorless.

What could I do? Slap something together and toss it back to the boss man, get the grenade away from me before it blew? Maybe I'd never get it. Maybe I'd get fired and be blackballed from ever finding another job, all those school loans hanging over my head. Still, a half-assed attempt would get me through the day.

So, that's what I did.

I typed so fast that my wrists hurt and I had to shake them to get it to stop. I just blathered like the boss man had. It was crap. It was garbage. But, it was all I had. An hour later I dropped it in an email and hit *send*.

Adrenaline wave over, I started worrying. What would happen when he saw it? Would it be obvious I was either incompetent or not even trying? My crap saved me, but just to prolong the situation.

"Hey!" The boss man popped in my door, leaning in like we were work buddies and he was dropping by to shoot the shit. That was when I noticed he had an elephant gun slung over his shoulder. I hoped it was a toy.

I reflexively grabbed at something on my desk, trying to look like I'd been working. "Hey," I replied.

He nodded his head, even though there was nothing to agree with. "So, I took a look at the filing. Great job. I told you it wasn't that complicated."

I blinked. "Thanks," I finally said.

"Drop by my office later." He winked. "I've got something else for you to work on." Then he popped back out again, gone as quickly as he had come.

I turned back to my computer. I still didn't know if it was all a scam or not. For some reason, though, I started thinking I should get a theme. I started thinking I should do something Greek. Maybe plaster columns and statues. Maybe even a toga.

HAPPY TRAILS

Suddenly it felt like I'd been kicked in the head by a mule. That's all I could remember, that moment of impact. It was like I'd spaced out and just woken up when kicked. There was no mule, though. There was a gun in my hand.

I almost jumped to get away from whoever attacked me, but there wasn't anybody there. Alone, I was kneeling on my living room floor in front of my TV. Piles of bone chips and goo were all around me on my tan shag-carpeted floor. The room was quiet since the TV was off though there was a bit of a ringing echo fading from the air. I looked at the gun again.

Wait, I wasn't completely alone. Lynette, an ex of mine, was asleep over on my blue corduroy couch across the room. She wasn't stretched out, not like she'd intended to sleep there. She was more slumped over, sitting up like she'd dozed off while watching TV.

Holding the gun, I tried to remember what had happened; what had I done?

There was a gun in my hand. My head felt like I'd been smacked by something big. There was gore all over the floor. Had I shot myself? Had I done it on purpose?

The living room was a mess. I could see crushed beer cans and paper plates of microwave mozzarella sticks and potato skins. I must have been having another late movie night or something.

I did that sometimes. I'd watch *Killer Klowns from Outer Space*, *Troll 2*, *Chopping Mall*, *Deathstalker II*, or something intentionally horrible like that. I'd have a feast of frozen snacks and some beer.

But why would I have tried to kill myself? I didn't even remember being particularly unhappy about anything. I checked, but there wasn't a suicide note anywhere. Why had I done it? Why had I done it with someone in the room?

82

I reached and felt a big hole on the back of my head. I didn't really feel any pain, but there was a hole. I wasn't really bleeding, and I couldn't feel anything in the front, but that hole in back felt huge. I was scared to touch it too much.

How bad was I messed up? Was I dying? Could I even be fixed?

I was blinking. I was breathing. My arms still worked. There wasn't any part of me that appeared to not be working anymore. Despite the hole, I appeared to still be functioning in every way I could think of. Still, that big of a hole had to have damaged something. Maybe I just couldn't tell what was wrong.

Maybe my head was why I couldn't remember anything. That part of my brain might have got blown out. It might have been in all that crap on the floor. Maybe I wasn't thinking straight anymore. It seemed like my mind was working fine, but maybe I just couldn't understand how messed up I really was.

Had it been about Lynette? I looked over at her, but it didn't seem likely. I didn't feel anything when I looked at her. There was no despondency, no crushing heartache.

What was going to happen to me? I didn't want to check close, but this was bad. I couldn't just forget it had happened; I had a hole in my head.

There was going to be hospitals and bills. People would scream at me—police and mental wards. Lockup. Was I maimed for life? Was I even going to live? I just couldn't tell. Whatever was going to happen, I knew it wasn't going to be good. It was going to be very, very bad.

Frankly, that's really what I felt. I didn't know why, but I wasn't all that freaked out that I'd tried to kill myself. Dealing with the consequences, though that scared the shit out of me. I just couldn't handle that.

How would I explain? I didn't even know what had happened. How was I going to pay for a hospital anyway? How was I going to be able to handle not walking or something like that? What life-changing disfigurement would I have to suffer through? I didn't even feel like I could handle the interrogation, much less anything else like that.

No, there was no way normal life was even going to be possible at that point. If I lived, I wouldn't be able to take the shit I was going to have to go through. And, if I was going to die from it, why suffer through all the shit first? There just wasn't any choice about it; for whatever reason I'd done it in the first place, I had to finish it.

I examined the gun, but it wasn't going to be any help. The barrel had peeled back in four jagged pieces. It looked like some kind of horrible industrial flower. I touched one of the pieces and it was still hot. It must have misfired or something when I first shot. Regardless, I wasn't going to be able to shoot myself with it again.

You know, I didn't even recognize the gun. I didn't remember owning one. There used to be a shotgun, but I'd sold that one time for beer money. Anyway, this was a revolver. It wasn't black, but it wasn't chrome even before the misfire. It just looked gunmetal. It wasn't really big, so I guessed it wasn't a forty-five, but it wasn't tiny either. Really, I didn't know a whole lot about guns.

I needed time to think. Could I even think? I didn't know; it felt like I could. There had to be something in the apartment I could kill myself with. I just didn't want any pain. I had to find something.

Lynette moved. I froze, thinking she was waking up. She'd see all of it and would definitely call the cops. I'd lost my chance. However, she just mumbled something about *pancakes* and shifted a bit before going to sleep a little deeper. I was safe, so to speak.

Still, I needed my apartment to be empty. I needed time to work, maybe get another gun. Running a car in a garage wasn't an option because I didn't have a car. Or a garage. Slit my wrists in the bathtub? I thought that could work, but it'd take time. I needed time by myself for that, or anything else really.

But how was I going to be alone? I was sure I could get her to go if I woke her up, say she was too tired for hanging out and needed to go home, but not if she saw the hole while I was talking. How could she not see that? How would she not see the mess on the floor? She'd be sleepy, but not that sleepy. She'd freak right out.

I had to clean up. I hid the gun behind the VCR; that was the easy part. The goo was harder; I scooped it into a pile with my hands. For the lack of anything better, I jammed it back into the hole in my head. What could it hurt at that point, right? Then I tried to hold it all in by forcing this light straw cowboy hat I found on the floor over it.

The cowboy hat puzzled me too. Was it mine? Where would I have got it? I would never have owned something hick like that. The straw wasn't exactly beat-up or anything, but it was definitely well used. I couldn't understand the hat, but there was nothing for it. I'd have to use it and hope for the best, use it to hold my head together for a couple minutes. I could try to figure out why I had it later if I ever actually needed to.

Really, it didn't look as bad as you might think. Like I said, there wasn't a whole lot of blood. It seemed like I'd got up all the brains and bone and stuff. The hat hid the hole pretty well, too. It wouldn't pass a close inspection, but maybe it wasn't going to need to. All I needed was thirty seconds for a shove out the door.

I swallowed. I guess that still worked too. Then I walked over to where Lynette slept on the couch. All I could do was just wake her and give it a shot. I shook her shoulder lightly. "Lynn," I said as she opened her eyes, "you fell asleep. We should probably call it a night and have you get on home. It's pretty late." I smiled.

THE BOYS OF VOLUNTEER FIRE TWO-TWENTY-TWO-POINT-FIVE (AND A HALF)

Something happened the other day that got me thinking—is Allen Funt dead? Does anybody know? I can't remember and it's bugging the heck out of me.

You think I'd know that sort of thing though I guess I don't. I swear I heard something about him passing years back, but I can't be sure. I might just be remembering thinking about it. Maybe he's just in Miami somewhere. Still, it seems like he should be dead.

I mean, he was an old guy back when they did that *Candid Camera* show in the eighties. He was at least as old then as I am now, and old Billy boy—me—was a younger guy in those days. Sure thing he's got to be gone now.

Or you never know. Maybe he's still kicking. Some guys you assume must be dead and then you find out they're still hanging around someplace. Really old, but not worm food like Merle Haggard. After all, you can't keep track of everybody. Some days I just count myself lucky if I can be sure I remembered to put on pants before leaving the house.

It was those firefighter boys that got me thinking of old Allen. I hadn't been doing a whole lot before that, just flipping through a paperback tome of the most perceptive commentator on American society ever. That's right, Don Martin. Good old Fonebone was about to offer me some insights on US ingenuity by way of a snake-in-a-can type gag when somebody pounded on my front door.

Now, not being the rude sort by nature, I set the wisdom of Professor Martin on the end table and went to answer it. When I opened up, though, I got knocked down and three firemen burst through the door into my living room.

"Where's the fire?" the tall and bony blond one demanded. "Where's it at?"

Mind you, they didn't look much like firefighters to me. They had fire coats and hats and all, but that was all over blue jeans and white Fruit-of-the-Loom T-shirts with names scrawled in black marker. From that, Bryan was the blond scarecrow. Wayne was a fat young longhair kid and Nelson was a tiny little Mexican guy. At least, that's supposing that they wrote their own names on their shirts.

Nope, they certainly weren't up to any classy kind of dress. Not like me, striped collared shirt with suspenders and my best seed cap. Then again, not everyone can aspire to be on the cover of *GQ*.

"Fire?" I said. "There's no fire."

The fat kid had me a mite nervous. He was swinging around this big ax. It might have looked like something from a Shakespeare in the park set instead of a fireman's ax, but it was still an ax.

"Fire could be anywhere. Wayne, locate the source. Nelson, preventatively soak the area," the blond stick man ordered.

"Got it chief," the Mexican half-pint agreed, pulling in a hose that looked suspiciously like it came from my garden. He turned on the tap and started flooding my couch.

"Right chief," the tubby kid also responded, swinging his ax above his head.

Frankly, I would have been more worried about pudge with the ax than short round with the water, but tubs tossed the ax aside and plopped down on the couch. In fact, he got comfy right under the waterfall that pint size was spraying. Butterball didn't pay it any mind, though. He just grabbed my remote and started watching TV. I think it was the old *Family Feud*.

"Now look here," I said, but then I didn't know what to say after that. Nelson kept going with the hose, looking a bit bored, and Wayne watched TV underneath the uninterrupted flow of the cascading water.

That's when I started thinking about Allen Funt. I mean, I was sure I was on *Candid Camera*. That was the only explanation for all that crazy stuff. The crew just wanted me to bug out so they could get a good bit of tape for the show.

Of course, I wanted to oblige if that was what was going on. They worked hard for the setup and I wouldn't have wanted to spoil their bit. I didn't want to look like a fool, but all their prep was for nothing if I spilled the beans on camera.

Still, that was only if those guys were from *Candid Camera*. Was that show even on the air anymore? I wasn't sure. It'd been a long time since I'd seen it, but maybe it was still playing on one of them high-up cable channels I didn't get. I tried to think, but it wasn't getting me anywhere.

Heck, I was pretty sure Allen Funt was dead. He'd probably passed on years ago. I wasn't any surer about that than anything else, but it seemed like there was no show if there was no Allen.

But didn't they do another show just like it? I think that Kutcher kid hosted that one. Maybe I was getting *Pranked* or whatever they called it, although I thought that show got canned too. Maybe the Kutcher kid was dead himself.

I'm telling you, the more I thought it through the less I could be sure of it. Next thing I probably wasn't going to be sure that even I was alive anymore.

"Clear the exits," boney Bryan bellowed, standing straight as a fence post in the middle of my living room. "Check for smoke. Feel for heat spots."

I don't think Nelson and Wayne were even paying attention at that point. They sure didn't act like they were. Course, maybe Bryan wasn't shouting at them. Maybe I was supposed to do all that. He kept right on going, though, whether I did or not.

"Secure any victims inside the residence."

Bryan grabbed me like I was a sack of russet potatoes and slung me across his back. I thought for sure he was going to crumple, but the spunky beanpole stayed up. I guess crazy adds a bit to strength.

"Seek higher ground to get the victim out of smoke-filled areas," he yelled, charging up the stairs to my second floor.

"Put me down," I managed to screech through all the bumping and bouncing.

"If there is no path out of smoke-filled areas, attempt to get the victim out of the house," he continued, charging back downstairs again.

"I said put me down."

Nelson and Wayne apparently had no interest in assisting with my *rescue*. Nor, apparently, were they going to rescue me from my rescue. They just kept on with their TV watching and sofa watering.

"If the exits are blocked—"

"Put that man down," a new, authoritative voice ordered from the direction of my open front door.

When I hit the floor, hard, I looked up to see a real fireman standing in my doorway. Full gear this time. The real deal. Big guy too, chiseled out of granite or some such thing. His brass nameplate said *Jon*, but had *Rusty* next to it in brackets. Seemed like he might have been Korean.

"Now get the hell out of here."

The three *firemen* ran frantically around my living room, hooting like they were *The Three Stooges*. They even ran right smack into each other a few times like they were playing bumper cars on too much coffee. Then they ducked past Rusty and bolted outside.

"You okay?" Rusty asked.

"I suppose," I replied, using the oak banister to pull myself up. "What the heck is going on?"

If it was *Candid Camera*, then that would have been the moment to spring it. All he had to do was point me out where the camera was hidden. I just hoped I hadn't broken a hip. Though, he didn't look much like Allen.

"Volunteer Fire," he replied.

"Pardon?"

"I saw their car and figured you might need a hand." He pointed out the door at a beat-up black and gold seventy-nine El Camino the three jokers had packed into. The words *Fihre Trukkk* were spray-painted in white on the side. "It always gives them away."

"But—"

He held up a thickly gloved hand. "Don't get me wrong, there's a lot of damn fine volunteer fire fighters out there serving a lot of communities that can't afford anything else. A lot of people would be up a creek without them. But, then there's some who live where they aren't needed and just can't give up the dream. Those ones," he pointed behind him, "are just trouble for everybody."

Rusty tipped up the front of his hat just a bit with one hand. "You have my sympathy as to any damage those boys caused, but I'm afraid you won't be able to look to the department for any help. I'd have you sign a release, but they aren't affiliated in any way and we just don't have any responsibility for them. You'd best just clean up the mess yourself."

He turned and walked off, but I kept looking around for Allen. I didn't expect much to see him at that point, but it just would have made more sense.

Does anybody know if he's still alive or not? I really want to know.

THE DES MOINES KABUKI DINNER THEATRE

Helen stared at her dark-haired husband, dinner plate in one of her hands and bizarre note in the other. Shocked, she watched him sip his espresso and waited for him to speak. Instead, Renaldo ignored her as if she hadn't stopped washing the dishes. He smiled and licked the *crema* off his delicate lips as he finished before departing for his study.

The dinner table was bare except for the demitasse cup and saucer. With the dishes all in the sink where Helen was supposed to be mechanically washing them, all traces of Renaldo's marinated pigeon and fresh olive oil sautéed peppers were gone. The sight made Helen feel abandoned.

Noting the dribbling from the plate onto her matching torn gray sweats, Helen dropped the plate in the clouded soapy water and stared again at the note.

Despite the contents, she couldn't help notice how beautiful the note was. Flowing letters drawn like impressionist brush strokes, maybe with a fine fountain pen, on parchment-like stationary paper. The kind of paper Renaldo had used to send his relatives abroad an announcement of their wedding. But, the message was not beautiful.

She read again.

Oh, my perfect little pigeon. How happy you will make my wife with your wonderful tastiness. You are so different from the roast of last night's culinary sufferings. So overcooked. So tough. So flavorless. Is this how my Helen feels about me? That I am bland? That I am a tiresome thing that sustains mere life but does not exalt the soul? I worry, my careful creation. What is my Helen trying to tell my by presenting me with such a meal?

Helen shook her head in disbelief. It was ridiculous. A note? Stuck to the bottom of a plate where she'd be sure to find it?

91

Renaldo wouldn't do that to talk about something so serious. It was too much of a joke.

Admittedly, Renaldo did not generally talk about problems openly. Confrontation was vulgar; Helen guessed he thought that although he had never specifically said so. Even at office parties, he'd never correct anyone who introduced him as the company's Spanish interpreter. He would just smirk and then snub that person forever after. Renaldo spoke *Castilian,* and only *a fool* didn't know the difference.

Still, reserved or no, this was her. He told people she was his *artist,* even though she sold deliberately crude birdhouses thrown together from scavenged scrap wood. They'd always had that connection beyond words, ever since the lit course back in their college days. She'd read the assigned stories to him because his English was so new and he couldn't follow. He couldn't resort to such odd ways to communicate with her.

Scrunching her face in the way she knew made her look ugly, she *hmmphed* and threw the note in the trash. It really was a joke. That was all, a playful little joke. He wasn't serious. Not her Renaldo.

Then Helen dutifully scrubbed the dishes. The joke was cute, but that was about it. Cleaning the dishes was still necessary. It may not have been as *carefully perfect* as the pigeon, but it was her contribution to the meal. She and Renaldo took turns cooking and the other always cleaned up. That was their way, their partnership.

But, two nights later, when it was again Renaldo's turn to cook, another note waited for Helen on the bottom of Renaldo's plate. Renaldo had already gone upstairs to make an international call to the family back home, so Helen immediately snatched the note and read.

My suckling lamb, though Helen enjoys you with me, I think that there are really only two of us at this meal this evening. My wife may dine with me, but her thoughts seem far away from me. The spaghetti of the night before leaves me no other thoughts to think. The noodles, so underdone. Though they bent with the softness of a light caress, each bite had a hard crunch like a slap and a raw starch flavor of neglect. Did my Helen rush the cooking so she could later meet a lover? Is there anything else for me to believe from this?

Helen balled up the note in her fist and threw it at the wall. She nearly threw the plate after it, or at Renaldo. Nearly stormed upstairs and broke it over his head while he trilled pretty foreign sounding sweetness to his aging mother.

She fumed, clenching the dirty plate. He knew she wasn't the world's greatest cook. Helen never pretended any different. Renaldo may have had flair and finesse in the kitchen, but she was more limited and made no secret of it. Roasts and spaghetti were her best though better than the TV dinners from before they had met, and her best was sometimes over or undercooked. Why would he act now like that failing meant more than it did?

Scouring the dishes with much more strength than necessary, Helen wanted to scream at Renaldo. Demand an explanation, force him to confront this head on instead of hiding behind clever little notes.

But Helen knew Renaldo would not say a word if she charged in like that. His way was to sidestep gracefully, like a matador. Only a bull met such a charge head on. A matador, however, would simply not be there anymore.

Helen sagged and rinsed the dishes before dumping them in the drying rack. So what was she to do? If she couldn't force Renaldo out of his little game, what could she try? Cook better so he wouldn't think she didn't love him anymore? Learn to be fancier about it so he wouldn't notice her mistakes so easily?

Is that what he wanted from her? Didn't he know she would have done all that before if it were possible? Wasn't her cooking proof that it wasn't? After five years?

With no more dishes, Helen felt helpless. She couldn't go to Renaldo because she hadn't figured out how to respond. There was a distance between them for some reason and she would feel it all the more if she was close to him. Instead, she went to the garage.

The garage was hers. Her workshop, a place Renaldo never went. He never even parked his car there. They both didn't, what with all her tools and discarded logs and lumber found in dumpsters or at roadsides. Between the half-built birdhouses, fasteners, and other junk items that might one day be useful, there was room for nothing else there but her. It was a sanctuary, but all she wished was that she didn't need one.

Helen picked up a recent work—a house assembled from two by four leavings recovered from a construction site trash heap. It looked like a clumsy jigsaw puzzle with perhaps a bit of

Frankenstein's monster thrown in. Not sanded, uneven, not even symmetrical, it was far from pretty or elegant.

Still, that was the point. That was why some rich idiot would give her fifty or even seventy-five dollars for the worthless thing. Her houses were supposed to look like they lacked craftsmanship like they were made out of garbage. Then the buyers could feel smug that they were doing their part, like the carbon offsets and other frauds they willingly fell for. They felt good and she got good money for no more than twenty minutes work. No one expected anything more of her.

So why did Renaldo all of a sudden? She made the gesture like she was supposed to; she cooked for him when it was her turn. As usual, it wasn't good. When did that start to mean that her feelings weren't adequate? Was the food even the problem? Or, was it perhaps something else and this was all just Renaldo's way of dancing even further around the reality? Would things be fixed even if she suddenly could cook for him the way he did for her?

Helen sat with her plain face in her rough hands. It was hopeless. She had no idea what was really wrong and no idea at all how to fix it. Renaldo would be lost to her, like he was on the other side of the water in a departing boat, waving handkerchiefs to tell her things in a pattern she couldn't understand.

She looked down at the makeshift house on the shop table in front of her. Though it was finished and ready for sale as it was, she started pointlessly sanding it. Her need to do at least something wouldn't let her be.

The next night, though, Helen chewed the last bite of her adequate ham and watched Renaldo at the sink. The thrill of sneakiness electrified her, but she tried to be patient. She wanted to pull it off just as he had done, but for that she couldn't rush things. She had to wait.

Renaldo scraped ham grease from the baking dish into the trash, his dinner dishes already ready to be washed. Helen had deliberately eaten slower than him, watched him, carefully looking for her moment. It wasn't until he cleared his portion of the table that she would have her opportunity, so she had to make sure she was still eating when he was through. Without, of course, dawdling obviously. The whole thing would have been up if she had been obvious.

The ham hadn't been anything special. She hadn't even done the improbable and made sure it wasn't too dry. She knew it would be, and it was. Helen had accepted this. Even the au gratin potatoes were from a box and would have been better if she had stirred more frequently. It had been dinner and it had been fine, but nothing particularly more than that.

No, Helen had hatched a different plan while doing useless things to that birdhouse. She had thought of it and then waited for her chance. As Renaldo had run water for the dishes and used the sprayer to make the soapy water foam, she'd noticed he wasn't looking and stuck a note of her own to the bottom of her plate.

She still wasn't sure why she had done it. It had just felt right. No more able to replicate the elegance of Renaldo's ones than she could his dinners, she'd written her own in cheap ballpoint pen on the back of a Safeway receipt. It read

Dear Ham,

What is bothering Renaldo? I thought maybe you would know since you were going to be spending time with him tonight. He has always taken me as I am, never wanting me to be someone else, and I love him for that. But, lately I feel that he has forgotten me and thought of someone else in my place. Suddenly, the things I do are taken to say words I never wanted to say. Maybe my husband and I are losing touch. That thought scares me. I want nothing more than to be as close to him as we have always been. Can you help me, Ham?

Helen's heartbeat raced. She was sure Renaldo had to know what she was doing even if he pretended he didn't. It wasn't as if she was sly. She wasn't; she knew that. Regardless, whether Renaldo saw through her or not, he acted as if he didn't have a clue.

At his place at the sink, Renaldo gracefully turned at the waist. Seeing her empty plate, he reached toward her. Helen gulped and then smiled, getting up to hand him her dishes.

Their eyes locked briefly. It felt like the time before they'd dated when he *happened* to run across her at the dance club. Her friends had dragged her there and she hadn't been having a good time, but he'd caught her eyes and claimed her on the dance floor.

At the instant both of their hands were on the plate, Helen saw Renaldo smile as his fingers felt the note on the underside. Her fingers withdrew and she held her breath as he peeled off the note. He read, not hiding the note at all, and smiled again. He'd got her to play his game.

Suddenly, like the graceful matador's stab after the bull is distracted by the cape's pass, Helen shot her arm out and smacked Renaldo across the back of the head. "Now cut the crap." She yelled. "And talk to your damn wife."

After all, she wasn't going to do *everything* his way.

TURNDOWN SERVICE

Margaret's heels clicked repetitiously on the polished marble floors of Finklebean's Mortuary. The sharp sound echoed down aisles of metal-faced vaults in the chilled, solemn hallways. Her steps were quick but purposeful, her stride constrained by the tight skirt of her starched navy business dress. An invoice was clutched tightly in her talon-like hand. Someone owed her an explanation and that debt would be paid.

Catching sight of the plain brown wooden door hidden off in a back hallway bearing a faded *Caretaker's Office* sign, Margaret halted, causing her heels to clack loudly on the stone. She pursed her lips as she scrutinized the sign. As if using the white metal sign with flaking black letters as a mirror, she adjusted the smartly coiled chestnut bun of her hair. Then she shoved open the weathered door and marched inside.

"Excuse me," she called out sternly before looking at what the room happened to contain, or even whether it was occupied.

A portly man in old blue coveralls sitting at a rough wooden worktable looked up at her calmly. Long stringy gray hair framed his face around a set of coke bottle eyeglasses perched on the end of his reddened bulbous nose. A metal cart, half full of plastic funeral flower arrangements, was positioned next to the worktable. Individual plastic flowers littered the table surface.

Unlike the somber and silent polished gray marble trimmed in shining brass of the hallway outside, the caretaker's room felt more like a basement or garage. The walls were cinderblock, unpainted, and the floor was bare concrete. Obviously, the room was not used for professional services.

"My bill is incorrect," Margaret said, thrusting the invoice out at the frumpy little man between a thumb and forefinger, both with nails bearing a French manicure. "You maintain my grandfather's plot, but this month's bill is way over the usual twenty-five-sixty-three. Nine hundred dollars more to be precise. You may not be the person in charge of this, but you're who I found."

The older man quietly looked at her still presenting the invoice even though he had made no move to take it. "Name?"

"Margaret Lane," Margaret said curtly.

"No," the caretaker shook his mess of oily old hair. "I won't remember you. I meant your granddad's."

Margaret pursed her lips again. "Winston Lane."

"Ah, yes." The heavyset man leaned back in his chair, putting his hands behind his head and cocking out his elbows. His belly pushed on the table slightly, causing loose plastic flowers to roll around on the tabletop. The flowers were separated into piles according to color, red, white, yellow, purple, and orange. "Winston Lane. His is over on hillside four, I believe."

"I'm sure." Margaret crossed her arms, still clutching the invoice. "So why do I have a bill for over nine hundred dollars?"

The caretaker hunched forward, setting his chin on a pudgy arm and wrapping a flabby hand around his mouth. "Let's see. Winston Lane. Bigger than normal bill. . . oh, that's right." His face brightened with recollection.

Margaret smugly waited for the expected rationalization to begin, the extras and add-ons designed to take advantage of the gullible grieving. She wouldn't be so easily manipulated.

"He got an apartment."

Margaret's expression cracked.

"That's what the extra money is," he pleasantly explained. "It's to cover the rent."

Margaret stared, blinking occasionally. A thin purple vein throbbed angrily at the side of her neck.

The man smiled. Then he pushed his round glasses further back up his nose and grabbed one of the plastic funeral arrangements from the cart. It had a block of dense green foam set in a fake bronze vase and various colors of plastic flowers stuck in the foam. The man pulled all the flowers out in a single movement and set each in the respective colored pile on the worktable. Then he placed the vase in a pile of similar vases on the floor.

"You rented my grandfather an apartment?" Margaret finally asked. "Why?"

"Don't be ridiculous," the older man snorted, dismembering another arrangement. "He rented the apartment, not us."

Margaret sneered, having recovered her self-possession and indignation. "Sir, my grandfather is deceased."

"Yep," the caretaker agreed. He started quickly taking vases from the cart, ripping them apart, and then tossing the materials in the respective sort piles. "Guess he didn't like the plot he picked out. Maybe it wasn't roomy enough, I don't know. Some things like that you just can't be sure of 'till you get in a place and stay there a while. Anyway, he must not have liked something about it because he went and got himself that apartment. He wouldn't have done that if he'd been happy where he was at."

Margaret stood rigid. The toe of one foot tapped irritably. "How could my grandfather possibly rent an apartment? He's dead."

"How couldn't he?" the caretaker snorted again. "It's a great apartment. Plenty of light. Nice carpets. Good amount of space. It's got a nice pool, too. Not that pools make much of a difference to a guy like him, being dead and all. Anyway, take a look; happen to have a photo of the place right here. Can't rightly remember why."

The man handed Margaret a bent-up photograph he pulled from a coverall pocket. It depicted a pleasantly lit living room with vaulted ceilings. Tasteful black leather and chrome furniture was arranged around a delicate glass coffee table. On top of the coffee table sat her grandfather's mahogany coffin, looking just as stately as it had at her grandfather's funeral service.

Margaret glowered, unsure what to make of the photograph, noticing after a moment that she was chewing her lip as she ground her teeth. Her brain couldn't keep up, it was all just too ludicrous for her to grasp. The man sorted more funeral arrangements. "So you're telling me that my deceased grandfather rented an apartment. Him, not you."

"Yep. That's the long and short of it." The man jammed the photograph back into his pocket.

"My dead grandfather."

"Yes'm." He took the last arrangement off the cart and disposed of it as he had the others. He paused to dust off his hands. Then he grabbed a vase from the floor, jammed a plastic flower inside from each stack, and set the newly arranged arrangement on the cart.

"How could anyone rent my grandfather an apartment?" Margaret threw up her arms. "He's dead. The landlord couldn't do that."

"Sure they can," the caretaker countered, paying more attention to the funeral arrangements than Margaret. "The building is zoned for mixed use."

"Mixed use? He's dead." She wiped her hand down her face slowly, stretching her skin as it went.

"So? He's residing there. That's a residential use. Certainly isn't commercial." The caretaker accidentally shoved two red plastic flowers in the same vase. Laughing at himself, he ripped them out again and started over.

Margaret stepped back, perhaps wondering if the caretaker was insane as opposed to just conning her. That would explain the photograph.

She crossed her arms loosely and tilted her chin upwards just a little, trying to mentally get a handle on the situation. Her brain felt like an overheated car with no oil in the engine. "I'm sorry, but that's very distracting," Margaret commented, pointing at the plastic flower piles on the worktable. "Is there any way that you could stop a moment?"

"Sorry." The older man shook a thick calloused finger at an old clock on the wall, stopped as far as Margaret could tell. "I got to get this done."

"But what exactly are you doing? You're just taking them apart and putting them back together."

The rumpled man gestured at the flowers. "Well, people pay us to put these on graves, don't they?"

"Right."

"They come from a factory, don't they? Someone paying someone else to bring something a machine made? I don't think much of that. My way, there's at least *some* thought in it."

Margaret did not respond. Instead, she watched the man fill up the cart again. The arrangements looked exactly the same as before.

"Anyway," the caretaker went on, "don't you owe your granddad?"

"Pardon me?" Margaret puffed out her chest.

"Sure," the man said, peering up at her through the finger-smudged lenses of his glasses. "He said when he bought the plot that you were going to take care of it and he was going to leave you money to keep going to school. He thought you should start working, but helped you out since you were going to mind his spot."

Margaret swallowed, ruining her attempt to look indignant. A few beads of sweat gathered at her temples.

"You figure you've done enough?" The man had his head held low, hiding the tiny smirk on his face.

Margaret's eyes widened. Her arms hung limply at her sides and her shoulders slumped. "But—"

"Hey, that's between you two. I just take care of things like I'm paid to. If he wants his plot, I do that. If he wants a two-bedroom palace, I do that instead."

Margaret absentmindedly twisted an old, ornate gold ring on her finger. Suddenly, her eyes narrowed as if the light in the dim room had got brighter. The meticulously squared corners of her mind twisted and stretched deliciously. "That's right, it was a deal."

"Come again?"

"I agreed to have his plot cared for."

"And?"

"Well." Her lips slipped into a pointed grin. "I pay you a fixed monthly amount to care for that plot. Apparently, this apartment is his plot now, so the rent should be part of your monthly care. I expect you to take care of it accordingly. After all, caring for his plot is caring for his plot."

"Now see here—"

"Regardless, I can't help but think," she went on, "that it reflects poorly on your services if grandfather isn't happy with his plot, not mine."

The caretaker gawked at Margaret, his mouth hanging loosely. "Is that what you think now?" the older man finally growled.

"It is," she responded with a saccharine tone, "and I expect that all future bills will be for the correct amount."

"Hmph," he huffed, settling back into his chair. "Wonder what your granddad would say about that."

Margaret smirked. "You're welcome to go and ask him if you think it will get you anywhere."

DREAMS OF DEAD GRANDPA

Personally, I think it's important for every boy to have a relationship with his grandfather. That sort of thing connects him to his past, lets him know how where he comes from joins to where he's going. Give his life a bigger context, you know? Me and my dead grandpa have that sort of thing. I guess. At least, it's more than we really connected while he was alive.

I mean, who we all are is in some way a reflection of the past, right? At least somewhat? Sure, we all think we're out here on our own. But the more we find out about who our parents and grandparents were, the more we start to wonder. The past at least forms a foundation for our lives and we might as well know what that foundation is made of.

My grandpa and I just didn't know each other real well while he was still around. I mean, he was old since I could first remember, at least since I was a little kid. I never approached him much because of that, and because he was always angry. I'd heard things about him, but we never really talked.

I just always kind of thought of him as this worn-out, mean old guy. One of the adults usually talked to him when I was around, and they usually weren't too happy about it. Other than that, he'd just smoke at the table in the kitchen or recline in his brown tweed easy chair in the living room. Sometimes he'd take naps and we did everything we possibly could to make sure he didn't wake up. That stipulation was made very clear to us. *Don't wake up grandpa.* Then we'd leave and I wouldn't see him again until we drove down to my grandparent's house a couple months later.

We didn't live in the same city.

It was hard for me to think about him the way people said, though I could picture the screaming career military part. I could imagine him yelling and standing at attention. Honestly, he was always kind of an asshole, and even still cut his hair in a flat top, what there still was of it. Even just talking, he sort of barked. Worn-down or not, he was clearly an angry guy.

The jazz musician part of him was harder to fix in my head though that part hadn't surfaced since his twenties. I also had a hard time picturing the math whiz, the home engineer automating his HVAC systems from a little cinderblock room in the basement. I just couldn't reconcile any of that with the grandpa I knew, but it's what I was told.

Frankly, the closest I got was when he made everybody listen to John Philip Sousa records in the living room, endlessly at high volume because he was almost deaf. There just wasn't much else at that point.

By the time he'd died, I'd moved across the country. It was a second heart attack, so there was no real surprise involved. We all knew it was coming; I'd just gone away by the time it actually happened. Still, it felt weird not being able to go back for the funeral—my first big disconnect from the family.

There had always been this distance between my grandpa and me, this sense that we had to prepare ourselves before even saying *hello*. The tone was formal, as if we couldn't talk without a reason behind it. Missing the funeral just made the disconnect more obvious.

Maybe that's why I had the dream about dead grandpa, some sort of guilt thing most likely. Maybe I was just ashamed that I didn't *feel* more and didn't go back, something that just bubbled up to the surface.

No. I take that back. It couldn't have been that simple. One thing I was certain about is that it really was dead grandpa. It definitely wasn't just a dream. I *can* be certain of that much.

I dreamed that I was back at my grandma and grandpa's house helping straighten stuff up. It was as if I'd been able to go back after all and was lending my grandma a hand. At the most important moment in the dream, I was putting a stack of towels away in my grandma and grandpa's bathroom, the one located off of their bedroom.

Of course, the room didn't really look that much like my grandparent's real bedroom. I actually hadn't gone in there enough to remember what it looked like. In the dream, the bathroom was almost just a part of the bedroom—just down a small set of stairs from the bed instead of being a separate room sectioned off by any walls. My grandparent's bed towered above the little staircase like a throne, hulking.

As I walked down the stairs, clutching the towels, I felt exposed, vulnerable. It seemed like I was the focus of the whole room, as if it was all bearing right down on me. It even felt like I was being watched, glared at.

Instantly, in the dream, I knew my dead grandpa was watching me. I could feel him. I knew he was on the bed, looking at me, and I knew that he knew I knew. I turned toward the stairs to face him.

Somehow, even though I knew he was there the whole time, I still screamed when I saw him. He was sitting upright in the bed, half-covered by a sheet as if he'd just been taking a nap and sat up when I walked in. He wore those white and blue type of striped pajamas that old men always wear though I had no idea whether my grandpa ever actually wore those or not. In any case, I screamed.

And when I screamed, my dead grandpa screamed, too. He wasn't scared like I was, though. He screamed like he was trying to scare me, and even maybe like he was trying to do it without cracking up laughing. I got the idea that he thought it was funny to scare me and was even funnier that I was actually scared, but wouldn't be funny if he laughed and fucked it up—like that would spoil the whole gag. Maybe it was part scream and part scream-laugh.

That was when I woke up.

I realized I had been dreaming, but I was sure I hadn't *just* been dreaming. It felt different than a normal dream; it felt like it really had been my dead grandpa. I was completely convinced it was him.

Of course, I was baffled why my dead grandpa visited me instead of somebody he was actually close to. It wasn't like we even really talked that much or anything.

Still, even though he'd been trying to scare me, it seemed like he'd been reaching out. Maybe he was sorry that we didn't know each other well while he was alive. Maybe he wanted to do something about that and just didn't know how. Perhaps it was that scaring me was just how it all came out. I mean, he never really was very good at relating to people.

Then again, maybe he just wasn't as repressed beyond the grave as before. Maybe it just seemed like a good joke and he picked me for it. I didn't know for sure, but I was sure it was him.

Either way, the dream stuck with me. It didn't happen again, but I didn't forget it either. I could remember the moment of the scream as if it had just happened though it was only scary in the dream. Afterward, it just seemed silly.

Almost a decade later, I moved back to the middle of the country again. Obviously my grandpa wasn't there anymore, but my grandma still was. She wasn't doing too good at that point, but she was still around. She even still lived in that same house. For her, it was like nothing—or almost nothing—had changed.

Some wives just get weak and pass on within a year of their husbands. I don't know if it's from grief or just a lack of living without a separate identity, but you always hear about it. Some people think it's romantic, but it seems sad to me. My grandma, however, wasn't like that. Grandpa died and grandma went right on with what she was doing, barely missing a beat.

I'm not saying she didn't miss him, mind you. I'm sure that she did; she was married to the guy for a long, long time. I'm sure she felt all kinds of things. I never asked, but I'm sure she grieved and all that.

Regardless, my grandma was there when I got back. Though, I didn't see her very much even then. She hadn't kept up all the big family holiday celebrations we used to have. At first, after grandpa died, everybody still went down and my grandma just didn't make a big production out of it. No more turkey dinners and whatnot. Then, however, fewer people came down and my grandma held them less often. No more Easter, or Fourth of July, just Christmas and Thanksgiving. She just started setting out bread and lunchmeat instead of cooking anything. Eventually, she served nothing at all and people just went to the closest and only Runza in town. At that point, people just went down to check on her and make sure she was still eating.

Finally, she died. Stroke this time, she hadn't been as tightly wound as grandpa. It took her a while, slowly getting thinner and frailer until she had her final stroke.

Of course, I only heard about all that second-hand. My dad and his sisters had been the only ones going down to keep an eye on grandma. Nobody else was really necessary. My grandma and I hadn't been real close to each other either though there wasn't the distance like there had been with grandpa and me.

To be honest, my grandma was always kind of a wood-like German as long as I'd known her. She was friendly enough, but not much for frills or sentiment. Almost fatalistic, complete with bushy fifties black hair, giant plastic glasses, and brightly colored polyester pants in various hues.

She always told this one story about breaking her arm when she was a kid that I thought summed her up pretty well. Come to think of it, I don't even remember the part of the story about how she broke it. I guess that part wasn't particularly important.

The real story came after that.

You see, there was no doctor anywhere around where my grandma grew up. The closest thing they had was a veterinarian, God only knows why they had one of them, and so her family took her to see him. He set her arm all right, but her great aunt didn't like the look of the vet. She ended up re-breaking my grandma's arm and resetting it herself at home. No anesthetic or anything.

The funniest part for me was how my grandma told the story like it was—at most—a minor irritant instead of an unforgettable trauma. I know it had been a long time, but still. She obviously hadn't been exactly fond of the experience, but she told the story the same way my dad talked about the time he got whipped for peeing in the hallway while sleepwalking. It was worth repeated complaint but wasn't exactly a horror story for her.

That was my grandma, condensed. Not much flustered her, not enough to break her out of her routine. Whatever came her way was just life on that particular day and that was that.

Frankly, we just didn't have too much to say to each other. We liked each other well enough, or it at least seemed that way to me, but we just hugged when we saw each other and not much else. At least, we did as well as she could with those artificial hips she had. It had been a while since I'd even seen her when she passed on. I guess it wasn't that important to visit while my family was just trying to keep her alive as long as they could.

Of course, I did get down for her funeral. All the remaining family came in for it. It felt like she was gone already, though, when I saw her in the casket, so I really didn't count that as *seeing* her.

I started wondering if I was going to have a dream of her ghost at some point. I didn't have the guilt about missing her funeral like

I did grandpa's, but repetition seemed appropriate. Besides, we were down at her house all the time at that point. We had to clean it out to sell it since everyone was gone. It seemed like a dream would happen since it was in my mind all the time.

It was weird; I was expecting the dream and actually had it. I usually don't dream things I think I'm going to, regardless how strong the premonition feels. This one I did, though, even if it was a bit different than I expected.

In the dream, I was down in the basement, cleaning out one of the metal cupboards my grandma used as a pantry. I had actually done that outside the dream. My grandma hadn't been able to get down to the basement for a while before she died, so things in there were pretty nasty, even if it was just cartons of macaroni and cheese, boxes of Bugles, rye bread, and stuff like that. Maybe the moldy bread made an impression since I was cleaning out the cupboard all over again in the dream.

As I was dumping junk from the cupboard into a plastic trash can next to me, I knew full well that I was dreaming. I remembered perfectly well that I'd already cleaned it out. I even remembered getting a dumpster for all the stuff inside the house that no one wanted and we couldn't donate. The house was completely empty. It was obviously a dream since I was cleaning the cupboard again when the house was already bare. Still, I don't know why, but I kept cleaning it out anyway.

At that point, I knew what was going to happen. My grandma's ghost was going to come walking down the stairs. Even though she hadn't been able to go down them while she was still alive at the end, she was going to come down them in the dream. She'd come walking down and I'd scream before waking up. I knew that, but I kept cleaning anyway.

Of course, that wasn't what happened. This wouldn't be as interesting if it had. Suddenly, I knew things weren't going to work out that way. Even before I heard the steps on the stairs, I knew I'd been wrong.

Keep in mind, I'd spent a lot of time in that basement as a kid. They had couches and a TV down there and it was where the kids all went while the adults sat around talking in the kitchen or living room upstairs. After all that time, I knew what my grandma sounded like coming down the stairs.

It wasn't her.

The step was too heavy for grandma, too plodding. My grandma always went real slow because of those fake hips, but this person was going slowly because of taking breaks. He was also wheezing as he came down, which my grandma never did. Only my grandpa wheezed like that.

I turned, like I thought I was going to in order to see my dead grandma's ghost, and watched my dead grandpa coming at me. I was frozen in fear, but I was also thinking *What the hell?* He'd been dead for years, what was he even doing there? Why wasn't I seeing my dead grandma?

I watched his face. He really had to make an effort to look scary instead of laugh. He also had to make an effort to walk, but he had to try hard not to laugh too. Obviously, he knew he was supposed to be dead grandma and he found that very funny. He still wanted to scare me, apparently, so he tried hard to hold it together. I really should have been laughing myself, but I was still scared. I really couldn't understand why, even in the dream.

Predictably—and I say that because I predicted it as I stood there—my dead grandpa stopped when he got to the bottom and screamed at me. It wasn't much of a scream, since he lost it and laughed, but I still screamed and woke up.

I was honestly dumbstruck. The first dream had been a bit spooky, but the second was just plain ridiculous. Why the hell would I dream of my grandpa's ghost when my grandma had just died? It didn't make any sense. Had my grandma become just a component of my grandpa in my mind? Was my dead grandpa going to show up in my dreams anytime that anybody died? Was that his *thing* now?

The whole dream just struck me as bizarre. It didn't chill and stick with me the same way the first dream had. It was just too comedic to be taken seriously, too odd, no matter how scared I'd been while it was going on. I kept thinking about it, but only because I kept trying to make sense out of it.

But, really, what could I do about it? It wasn't like I could sit down and confront dead grandpa and demand he cut the shit out or just to say if he really wanted something. The dreams had only happened twice. Anyway, I wasn't in control of them. Even if it kept happening once in a while, he'd just scare me and that would be it. Whatever it was all about it was just something I had to accept. I had to live with it.

Mind you, that wasn't the weirdest that dead grandpa got, not by a long shot. There was one other dream of that house that was far, far stranger. I dreamed that dream long after the house had been sold and we hadn't returned there again. That one was just fucked up. I'm sorry, but there's just no other way to put it. There hadn't been a hint of sense in the last one at all.

Since you need to know a few key details, there had been this girl. We'd been together for about a year, but things went bad between us. I was still stuck on her pretty bad even after it ended, but things weren't ever going to work. All we did at the end was fight. Finally, she moved out while I was gone one day. I came home to an empty apartment and that was it. We had originally arranged to meet that night to go out for Chinese.

Plans change.

I found out that the girl had moved in with some friends of mine. I still saw her once in a while after that, but eventually she moved away to marry some guy in Kansas. No one really knew what happened to her then; we just didn't hear from her again.

I suppose it took me a while to let go, though, because I dreamed about her from time to time. For some reason, one dream took place back at my grandparent's old house.

I dreamed that we were cleaning it out yet again to sell, though it had been cleaned and sold years before, but even in the dream the house was empty and I was alone. I don't know why, but I went back into one of the spare bedrooms and opened the closet. Inside I found clothes, my ex's clothes.

Instantly, in the dream, I knew the girl had come back to me. That was why she'd put her clothes in the closet, to signal to me she'd come back so I'd be prepared before she faced me. Then, when I saw her, I'd already know and could deal with it. It was going to be easier to handle that way.

I don't know why, but that didn't strike me as weird. Sticking clothes in a closet as a first step in an emotional reunion made total sense. It didn't even occur to me to wonder why she'd come back to me at my empty grandparent's house instead of the apartment we shared. It all just felt right. It should have been odd as hell, but it wasn't.

Standing there looking at her clothes, all I could feel was this immense warm joy. I felt like I was going to cry, my vision even blurred like I was crying, but it was all okay. I knew it was okay.

Ripping myself away from the closet, I ran for the kitchen. I knew she'd be there, washing dishes. I don't know why she would have gone to wash dishes, or where she would have even got dirty dishes to wash, but there you go. That's how she wanted me to find her after I found the clothes. She'd have her back turned and she'd be crying too. She'd be crying because she was so happy that I was happy she was back. It was just a dream but I really was happy.

In fact, when I got to the kitchen in the dream, she was standing at the sink crying and was washing dishes. She was so happy that she couldn't talk. She needed me to say something so the joyful reunion could burst open between us. I sensed this.

But, then she turned and suddenly she was my dead grandpa.

I'd seen the change as she/he turned, but I still looked around the kitchen to see where my ex had gone. I only saw my dead grandpa and I couldn't grasp the switch. It was like the dream with my ex suddenly stopped and I was in a totally different dream with my dead grandpa.

I stared at him. It was almost like he was waiting for me to catch up so we could get on with the dream. He just stood there and chuckled until I guess he thought he had my undivided attention. Then we did our screaming and I woke up.

Frankly, other than being completely confused by what my dead grandpa thought he was doing, I was kind of pissed. I mean, what the *fuck* was going on? No one had even died that time. Was he just going to show up randomly to freak me out? Was that all there was to the entire freaky situation? Was this his game?

It still had only happened three times, which wasn't a lot, but still. Dead grandpa just pops in once in a while, scares the shit out of me, and maybe ruins a nice dream or two. *Thanks, dead grandpa.* That's a fine way to spend one's hereafter.

Anyway, that's why I think it's important for a boy to know his grandfather and, from that, know more about himself. As for me, I apparently come from people who are willing to squander their afterlife on cheap jokes. A light at the end of a tunnel? Nope, not for us. Elysian Fields? No, thanks, we'd prefer to mess with those still living. Also, jokes like that apparently never got old for us.

Personally, I think this is an important thing to know about one's self. I owe that much to my dead grandpa, the fucker. I never would have guessed that sort of thing was in me and it's something I think I should really know about myself.

So, thanks, Grandpa. *Thanks a lot.*

THE ONION SHE CARRIED

Nan was awake, but her large frame stayed prone in her bed. Her alarm was going to buzz in just a few minutes, but she didn't slap at it with her oversized hand to shut it off. She didn't even open her eyes.

The day was just going to be the same thing as any other day. She was going to work. Then she was going to come home, watch TV, and go to bed. It was going to be just like the day before, and the next day would be no different. Though her muscles were stronger than those of the average person, Nan barely felt able to move.

But then, Nan decided something had flipped in her brain. Whether it had or not, she decided it had. The day was going to be different after all. That day was going to be an onion day.

The bed and floor groaned in turn as she rolled from the former to the latter. She lumbered into the kitchen and opened the crisper in the fridge. There was an onion all right, big and yellow, and slightly teardrop-shaped. Nan held it up high like a gigantic diamond and marveled at it. That onion would do nicely.

She set the onion on a prominent spot on the linoleum counter and had some instant coffee while she made breakfast. Then she carried the onion to the bathroom and rested it on the sink edge while she showered. She even took it with her when she pulled the clothes from her closet to get dressed, trading the onion from hand to hand when putting each respective ham of an arm through a sleeve.

It was, after all, an onion day.

Ready for work, Nan locked the front door of her single level house and plodded to the train stop. She clenched the onion in her hand like an apple carried by a hick kid to his pretty, young teacher.

Usually, Nan found a seat alone on the train. Everyone tended to, spreading out as much as possible by automatically picking the seat furthest from where anyone else was already sitting. No one who rode that particular train seemed to want to interact with other people in the mornings. That morning, though, Nan sat right across from a slightly older man. She put the onion on the seat next to her as if it was a separate passenger. The man looked out the window to avoid eye contact, probably ruffled by the breach of the unspoken etiquette.

Nan thought the man looked Indian. Then she reminded herself that he could just as easily be Pakistani, or Bangladeshi, or even a few other things for all she knew. Indian was just the first thing that came to mind, and she bet that it probably wasn't right.

He was kind of a fat little guy, she noticed. Nan was big, towering over him as she did most guys, but she wasn't really fat. She was built big, linebacker shoulders and all, definitely overweight, but she wasn't round and soft looking like the fat little guy. She imagined people would expect him to be jolly. No one ever expected her to be jolly.

"I've got an onion," she told him after the train started moving and it was too late for him to change seats. She held it up.

"I see," the man said politely but curtly, obviously trying not to say something open ended that would encourage further conversation.

"Today is an onion day."

The man nodded. She bet he worried about her being crazy but was too timid to actually do anything about his concern. She decided she could probably do just about whatever she wanted and he'd just let it go, hoping for her to lose interest or for the train ride to end.

She thrust the onion at him. "Want to touch it?" she asked, wondering just how much she could keep pestering him before he'd finally get up and move.

The man shook his head quickly and looked out the window, trying to ignore her. Nan smirked and put the onion back on the seat next to her. She wasn't going to waste all the onion on him.

Eventually, Nan's train arrived downtown. She got off and walked the remaining two blocks to work. When she got there, she mounted the onion on the corner of her cubicle wall, a place where anyone walking by in the aisle would see it. Then she started going through her morning email.

Throughout the day, she heard people walking behind her. She knew they saw the onion. She also knew they wanted to ask her about it, but no one did. No one stopped by and no one said anything.

When the time came for the afternoon meeting in the main conference room, Nan, of course, took the onion with her. She put it on the table right next to the pitch brochures they were there to talk about.

The city was building a new stadium over an old rail yard and Nan's firm was pitching to get some of the enviro work. The schmoozy, young office manager Fred wanted to brainstorm how they could better package themselves in the brochure to win the bid.

The entire idea bored Nan. Even the blond-office-tennis-pro look Fred had going on bored Nan. She knew her firm would either get the bid because they were cost-effective, had a reputation for solid work, and had the right contacts with the city, or they wouldn't. If it came down to image, then the bigger firms with outside marketing agencies would win no matter what the brochures looked like. Nan only wished she had spaced out, not paid attention to the little speech Fred gave about all the different players who had to be catered to and balanced against each other.

"How about you, Nancy?" Fred leaned toward her. "You've been quiet so far. Do you have any input?"

Everyone turned. She bet Fred thought he was clever to put her on the spot. Well, she was going to make him regret it.

"Actually," she responded, pulling herself all the way upright, "I do. I think the situation is just like this onion here." She reached and held up the onion for everyone. As she expected, they actually looked at it.

"Really? How so?"

"Think about it. This onion has all these layers, one inside another." She rotated the onion around as she talked. "There's all these different levels, but they're really all just the same thing. One layer isn't really any different than any other. All in all, it just isn't that complicated."

She set the onion back on the table and smiled.

Fred cleared his throat. "I see." He paused, "Does anyone else have any thoughts?"

When the workday was over, Nan rode the train home with her onion. She prepared for a night of television and a Hungry Man fried chicken TV dinner that she would enjoy with the onion as company. However, the more Nan thought about the idea, the more an evening at home seemed a waste of the onion.

Nan determined she needed to share the onion with more people, strangers. Luckily, she didn't have to go far. Nan didn't even know any of her immediate neighbors. She just lumbered down the sidewalk a block or two and started knocking on doors. When people answered, she showed them the onion. Then she shared the word of the onion with them, telling them about vitamins contained therein and little-known onion related health benefits. Whenever they closed the door, which sometimes happened later, but often happened sooner, Nan went on to the next house.

Only one house got a little nasty. That one only had the banged-up screen door shut, though she could see it was secured with a latch hook, so she couldn't knock. There was no doorbell either, so she had just called inside.

"What you want?" the wrinkled woman who came to the door snarled. She was wearing a stained plain white tank top. The view it revealed wasn't pretty. "I ain't buying nothing."

"I'm not selling anything," Nan replied. "I want to tell you about onions." She held her onion up for the woman to look at. "Did you know onions reduce cholesterol and can even prevent heart attacks?"

"Heart attacks? You coming around here telling me about onions and heart attacks? Are you stupid or something?" The bitter little woman squinted at her. "Tyrone," she screamed inside, turning back to look into her house. "I told you, no."

"Please, ma'am, there's nothing stupid about spreading the word about onions. The nutrients in onions don't get damaged when you simmer them. It just goes into the water. You can use them in soups and still get everything."

The woman snapped back, "Nutrients? Why you bothering me about onions and nutrients? You think I'm an idiot or something?"

"No, I just—"

"Get out of here," the woman said, smacking the screen door as if she was going to hit Nan. "I don't have time for this. Get out of here before I call the cops. Coming up to my door, harassing me about onions. This is my property and you can't just come on it."

Nan didn't wait for that particular woman to get mad enough to close the door. She just went ahead and left once the threat of police was raised. It didn't seem like it would be very amusing to talk to the police about her onion. Not that Nan was doing anything illegal, but Nan was wasting time with the woman; some people just weren't meant for onions.

Eventually, as the evening started getting late, Nan returned to her home with the onion, happy. She got ready for bed and placed the onion next to her alarm clock on her bedside table. Then, she fell asleep. The onion, of course, did nothing.

In the morning, Nan again awoke a few minutes before her alarm. She grinned and reached for the onion, expectantly.

Nan noticed that the onion looked a little darker, it's skin slicker. It gave off a sharp odor. Nan perceived that it was starting to rot.

It seemed odd to Nan that the onion had gone rotten so quickly. She'd just got it out the day before, after all. However, Nan noticed that the bottom bit, the disc-like part on the base where the little root ends came out, looked like it had been crushed a little. She must have set it down too hard at some point, tapping the base a good one. Nan thought she remembered something about onions immediately starting to rot when their bases got smashed.

Disappointed, she moved into the kitchen and threw the onion into the black plastic trashcan. For a moment, she just stood there, unable to decide what to do next. Things were boring again.

Suddenly though, she grinned and lunged for the fridge. That day was going to be a parsnip day.

CONTEXT DRIVEN

On the day of *the incident*, a young man with immaculately trimmed and gelled dark hair put on his turn signal and shot into the turning lane with smug perfection. He waited for a brief gap in traffic before swinging a wide left turn and forcing his way into the right lane.

"So Collard tells me he was making sure we were behind the team. Was there anything he should know before the boss checks in on things?"

"What?" a young woman in the passenger seat, compulsively fixing a loose strand of her platinum blond hair in the side mirror, exclaimed.

"He didn't come out and say it," the young man sneered, driving with one hand so he could make a self-important emphasis gesture. "It was all loyalty to the team. Now that things were bad, was anyone going to turn? He just wants to save himself."

"Wasn't it his plan? Didn't you say it was a bad idea?"

"Yeah. Now I'm right and he wants to stick together so the boss doesn't know," he said with his head turned, watching for an open spot. He flipped on his turn signal and jammed the car over into a small gap. A startled driver let out an angry honk. The young man flipped on his turn signal again and sharply turned into a parking lot.

"I hope you told him to shove it." The young woman said with superiority.

"Oh yeah. I told him I was loyal to the team, but I wasn't going to lie. Then I told him I didn't think the team was the problem." The young man gave a haughty nod of his head. "He knew what I meant."

The young man and young woman bolted out of the car simultaneously and marched around their respective sides toward a bookstore. Shortly after they each strutted out with a coffee.

"Where did we park?"

The young woman looked sharply around. "I think it's over there by that clunker."

Both got in, carefully buckling their seat belts. The man, rubbing absentmindedly at a spot on his head like it was a bald patch, which didn't work quite right since the spot wasn't bald, started the car. He checked the rearview mirror before cautiously backing out. The woman gently reached over and turned on the radio. Soft jazz lightly filled the car. Her hands reflexively went to fiddle with glasses on her face that weren't there, and dropped a second later when they didn't find glasses. The man politely waited for traffic to clear before turning out of the parking lot.

The man smiled beatifically and the woman smiled pleasantly back. "What was I talking about, mother? I'm can't seem to recall."

The woman looked sweetly thoughtful for a moment. "I think it was something about the firm. It was, wasn't it? I'm sorry, I don't really remember either. I must have had one of my little moments."

"Sullivan. That's what I was talking about."

"Of course, father. That was terrible that he got let go."

"It sure was, mother. He's been with us for thirty years, right from the beginning. No one cares about that firm as much as he does." The man eased the car to a stop at a red light. A second later, the light turned green and he paused before happily getting on his way so that a couple of turning cars from the adjacent parking lot could merge into the lane ahead of him.

"Wasn't there anything you could do?"

"He just couldn't handle the job anymore." He shrugged helplessly. "It isn't right, but business is business. No matter how much I didn't like it, the firm couldn't keep him around."

"It's still sad."

"It is, mother." He nodded regretfully. "I told him I would help any way I could. Give him a great reference if he needed it. Even offered to lend him a little money if he gets into a spot."

"That was nice."

"I owe it to him." The man glanced humbly over at the woman. "He gave me my start. That has to count for something."

118

The woman nodded in approval. The man gently drifted from the left to the right lane after checking his mirrors. He was pleasantly silent as he continued to drive straight ahead as if he was pondering something.

"This isn't right, is it, mother?" he said finally to the woman, smiling again.

"I don't think that it is, father."

The man checked traffic and carefully executed an overly wide U-turn around a cement island, driving back toward the bookstore. He pulled the car delicately but a little too closely into a spot next to another car. The other car was the same color and model. Another man and woman were standing outside the other car, grinning with polite amusement.

The young man and young woman got out.

"Looks like you mistook our car for yours." The other, older man laughed, rubbing the bald spot on his head. "I nearly got into yours myself."

"They're identical," the other, older woman smiled, causing her glasses to slip slightly. "I was waiting for father to let me in and I suddenly thought, my seat covers, where are my seat covers?"

"Sorry," the young man muttered, getting quickly into the other car.

"We're the Greenbergs, by the way," the other, older man said as he offered his hand through the other car's open door.

The young man reluctantly shook it. "I'm Brad. This is Sheila," he muttered. The woman sat stiffly with her arms folded over her chest.

"Nice to meet you both," the other, older woman replied sweetly.

"You folks ought to come to one of our dinner shindigs," the other, older man quipped, slapping his knee "This would be a hard story to beat."

"Sure," the young man replied sharply before slamming the door.

The other, older man and woman waved happily as the young man drove away. He angrily flipped on his turn signal and swung a wide turn out in front of an oncoming truck, speeding up just before the car was about to be rear-ended.

"Well, that was weird," the young woman finally grumbled, arms still crossed tightly. "I wonder what the hell all that was."

"What I can't figure out," the young man snapped without looking at her, "is how my key worked."

60% RAYON AND 40% EVIL

I fully acknowledge that I am a five-inch stuffed bear with a desire for murder. I understand this, never having claimed otherwise, and I understand this means I am quite different from the vast majority of humanity. I also recognize that due to this difference, I will likely never completely grasp why humans behave the way that they do. It is true and I admit it.

For the most part, I have no quarrel with this situation. My obsession is killing, not understanding. Regardless, you people really baffle me sometimes. My former owner, Tristan, baffled me more than most. I just never quite got that guy, and I doubt that I ever will.

Tristan originally bought me in Canada. According to my information, it was a tiny little gift shop in a Southern Alberta border town. Personally, I have no firsthand experience; I was not aware at the time of my purchase. I was merely a stuffed bear. All I know is what Tristan told me later though it is worthwhile to note that he did not know I was actually listening at the time.

He bought me for thirty-two dollars, Canadian. That likely equated to about twenty-four United States dollars back then. Taxes included. Tristan talked a great deal about taxes being included. For whatever reason, he could not get over how Canadians displayed prices including tax as opposed to guessing and being surprised at the register. I failed to see why that was significant, but perhaps it indicates something of interest about Tristan.

I sat in a closet for many years after I had been purchased.

Mind you, I did not mind being stashed for years at a time. I was not yet self-aware, so I was indifferent to being stuck in a closet or anywhere else. I am unsure why Tristan purchased me only to forget me for so long, but that is what happened.

Frankly, I am uncertain that anyone would have thought that I was anything but a cute, ordinary toy bear at that time. I was tan-colored, with lighter tan accents for my foot-paws, snout, and ears, though not my arm-paws, for some reason. I was soft and round-bodied with tiny limbs and an oversized round, head. My snout included a milk chocolate colored little triangle of a nose, point down, but my eyes were solid little translucent beads of deep, shining black. Looking into those eyes, perhaps someone would have been able to feel some dark indication of what I was to become.

Regardless, events did not become interesting—at least in my view—until Tristan rediscovered me when digging through his possessions while moving out of his parent's home. It was somewhere around this time, I am unable to say exactly when, that I first felt the stirrings of consciousness.

Perhaps Tristan had again seen some glimmer of whatever it was that spurred him initially to purchase me. Or, perhaps that transition to adulthood stimulated nostalgia for his child-times. In any event, Tristan decided I was something particularly neat when he found me again in that closet and picked me up.

He suddenly named me *Mr. Rictus* after a villain character in a Clive Barker novel and developed a whole persona for me where I had a fondness for killing. I believe *rictus* is a Latin word meaning something close to *jaws* or *open mouth*, which amused me since I have no mouth. He even carried me around with him, pretending to move me around as if I was animated and made up stories to tell people about my homicidal hobbies.

His favorite bit was to turn my head to a person and say to them, "Mr. Rictus wuuuuvvvvs you." That supposedly signified my decision to murder that person. Of course, he did not always disclose that fact, instead just performing the bit without necessary explanation, particularly to strangers on buses or ahead of Tristan in grocery store lines.

It should be clarified though I doubt anyone could be confused regarding this point from what I have related, that Tristan was by no means delusional. He believed none of these things. This was merely a game, a colorful affectation of weirdness, something quirky for Tristan to do in order to be a more interesting person—no different than when he cut the sleeves off of his denim jacket and continued to wear the cuffs. In no way did he really think that any of these things were true. However, strangely enough, and according to no mechanism that I at all comprehend, it all became true. In fits and spurts, I found myself becoming aware.

I was aware and able to move and driven by the desperate need to kill and kill and kill.

Reflecting back, I suppose it was amusing in a certain sense. Of course, I doubt the average person would be as amused as me, their lives generally being in danger as a result and all, but there is a certain humor in how events turned out if looked at in the appropriate context. Everything structured itself exactly as Tristan had been pretending.

For example, I did not demonstrate my changed status to Tristan. If I had been pressed at the time to explain why I did not, I believe I would have had difficulty precisely stating my rationale. The clearest way I can state matters, even now, is that it just didn't seem proper.

After all, it was a game, a theatrical trick, which Tristan had developed. The intent would have been spoiled if it had to be suddenly acknowledged as fact. One of the core features of Tristan's fiction was that I killed when no one, particularly him, was looking, so that is exactly what I did.

Keep in mind it was not as if I had to be crafty. Tristan was reasonably bright, but I doubt that anyone would have gone as far as to describe him as observant.

As much as he enjoyed playing his little game, he would often toss me into the bedroom corner by his thrift store dresser and space me off for random lengths of time. Then, just as randomly, he would pick me up again, carry me everywhere, and his fun would continue. His day-to-day activities took up a certain amount of time as well, and I was not always dragged along. Frequently, he would venture out for several days at a time to *get hammered*, only to finally return to his apartment and sleep for just about as long.

I found ample opportunities. As one might expect, I did take advantage.

Given the laxness of Tristan's supervision, I had little difficulty in finding time to surprise a young sociology professor in her bed late one night with a disposable shaving razor. I was also easily able to work in shooting a retired sheet metal worker during his morning walk with his own scoped hunting rifle from the window of his own spare bedroom. I even managed to get around to sealing a religious plasterwork enthusiast who made wall hangings of the Virgin Mary in his basement studio before setting the place afire.

Obviously, I proved quite resourceful.

One might not expect that a six-ounce stuffed animal would be able to accomplish a great deal, particularly in such physical-oriented activities. However, it was clearly unwise to make that kind of assumption. Events certainly proved that. I would elaborate on my methods and means, but my desire to convince is outweighed by my desire to retain the advantages I possess. After all, my *hobby* is ongoing.

Returning to the subject at hand—or paw—though, I should admit that I did become significantly less cautious about both my animated state and my violent enthusiasm as time went on. I had always acted according to the rules Tristan dreamed up, but I started following them in an increasingly less rigorous fashion.

I am unsure exactly why this was so. I do not think that I specifically considered the matter at the time, but this was what happened. It is possible that Tristan had become tired somewhat of the game and that correspondingly freed me from strict observance, making me less obligated to conceal. However, it is just as possible that I unconsciously realized that Tristan paid even less attention than I had previously imagined and acted accordingly. Whatever the true nature of the situation was, I definitely became more open.

I began disappearing while Tristan was home and did nothing to suggest valid reasons for my absence. People threatened with the usual "Mr. Rictus wuuuuvvvvs you!" vanished without a trace, or with only gory traces. Normally I obfuscated such things, things that should have tipped Tristan off, but at a certain point I had ceased to do so.

And, in Tristan's defense, he did eventually appear to catch on. He wasn't very observant, as I noted previously, but the boy wasn't brain dead.

It could have been my gradual replacement of apartment furniture with versions more suited to my diminutive size that finally got through to him. Then again, it could also have been my increasingly frequent habit of leaving bloody power tools in the metal kitchen sink with all of the usual dirty dishes. Whatever it specifically was, I noticed Tristan watching me more closely than he had before. There came a point where I was certain that Tristan knew everything, or, at least enough. He did nothing about the situation, but it felt clear that he knew what was going on.

Frankly, I suspect he simply had no idea what to do. I was a killer teddy bear and he was a Village Inn prep cook who took beginning psychology courses at a local community college. Simply put, he did not possess the necessary skills to stop me and did not try.

Personally, I thought we had a pretty livable arrangement in place. It was not as if Tristan had not seen any of the plethora of low-budget horror films on the market. It was obvious in light of such that I had no intention of going after him. He might not have been pleased with the way that the stars had aligned, but I was fairly certain he knew how he was to conduct himself.

But, then that cop showed up and proved my assumptions incorrect.

Really, this was simply an eventuality. I knew it would happen at some point, and I had definitely planned for that particular day. No matter how careful one is, and I had ceased being immaculately careful in any event, a trail would someday lead back to the apartment. As I mentioned, I was prepared for such.

After all, though there would be evidence, it was merely a trail. There was nothing definitive to be found out there. Sure, an officer was in the living room with his hands on his hips, saying something akin to *What's all this, then?* in a distrustful manner. However, an established way existed to handle the matter and the annoying pest would have had no choice but to pack up and leave.

For my part, all I had to do was sit there like the inanimate plush toy that I was supposed to be. For Tristan's part, he merely had to keep his wits about him and deny everything. The police had nothing specific on Tristan, could not since he was innocent, and they would never dream of arresting a toy. As long as we stuck to the *script*, we had nothing to worry about.

I expected that Tristan grasped this, but unfortunately, this was not how he proceeded. "He did it," Tristan said, snapping his hand up to point right past the cop toward me sitting in my orange vinyl padded wood teddy bear chair. "It was the bear."

I couldn't believe my ears if in fact my ears were what functioned to provide my hearing. What was he thinking? There was no way on earth the cop would believe him. Tristan had to have known that. He had seen the movies where correct and incorrect behavior for such happenings was set forth and analyzed in demonstrative detail. He surely understood, but he went ahead and acted to the contrary.

That's when the cop shot him, blasting Tristan in the chest with his forty-five semiautomatic. I don't know what Tristan expected, but pointing in a way that looked like he was pulling a gun on an already suspicious officer was certainly the *last* thing he should have done.

Predictably, I then killed the cop. I think that was understandable, particularly since I had to go through all the hassle of locating a new host. It was quite inconvenient.

Regardless, I never could fathom Tristan. It floored me then, and it still floors me to this day anytime I ponder it. Granted, I am a slaughter-obsessed children's toy allied with the menacing darkness skulking about the far edges of creation and I am not well-equipped to empathize with the minds of men, but I never understood and it has always troubled me. Colloquially put, you people *blow my mind.*

Perhaps that is one of the reasons I kill so many of you.

AN ENDLESS SERIES OF MEANINGLESS MIRACLES

Warren lowered his aging, pudgy body into the delightfully warm water of the claw-footed bathtub. Though he resembled more the short little guy in that *Up* movie than most of the kids he worked data entry with, he performed his meaningless job well and deserved a good soak at the end of the day. However, the fact that he saw the water level fall instead of rise as his body entered the tub shattered any relaxing effect that soaking normally had.

He instantly sat upright. Unfortunately, his body's motion splashed the tub water around, obscuring the evidence. All the sloshing swamped the water running down the tub sides from the pre-him position to the lower, post-him position.

Still, Warren was sure of it. The water level went down when he got in.

Hadn't it? He was already luxuriating in the heat of the water as he immersed himself, letting it engulf him. Could his attention have wandered? Was it possible that he was mistaken? Perhaps it was a kind of daydream?

No, Warren P. Forsmythe knew he was not a man who couldn't trust his own eyes. He had seen it; it had definitely happened. Warren was certain.

Further, Warren knew why such a thing was not what was supposed to happen when an object got into a tub. Mass displaced water. He remembered the story of Archimedes and his discovery, immediately followed by running naked through streets while shouting *Eureka!* The tub water had acted contrary to universal laws. Something unusual had happened.

However, Warren happened to overlook the fact that it was simultaneously unusual and completely unimportant.

Warren took his hand from the water and then lightly touched the surface. Nothing appeared unusual. It looked to be water; it was wet and had come out of the water faucet. Warren stared, but no explanation immediately suggested itself.

Carefully watching the sides of the tub, Warren curled a hand into a fist and thrust it deep into the water to try to recreate the anomalous effect. It wasn't any good, though. His hand simply wasn't big enough for Warren to detect a water level change.

He then braced a hand on each side of the bathtub rim and hauled himself out slowly. As he watched, the water level went down—just as he knew it was supposed to. He sunk back down and the water level rose again.

Warren scratched his head. Then he repeated the actions. Again, the water behaved normally—his body displaced it. He tried again.

In fact, Warren kept trying for quite a while. He wasn't sure exactly how long he'd been getting in and out of the tub, or how many times he'd done it, but he noticed that the water had gone fairly cold. The bath water retained some warmth, but enough time had apparently elapsed that the water was cooler than when he normally finished soaking. Despite all that activity, Warren had not once been able to recreate the reverse displacement he had witnessed.

Tapping a finger on the tub edge in thought, he sank as deeply into the bath water as he could go. He was determined to not waste the little enjoyable water heat that remained. After all, a day without some kind of soak was inconceivable.

Warren stewed with his thoughts. Though he had not been able to replicate the effect, he was still certain that it had occurred. He knew he had seen it, and he doubted it could have been delusion since he was sane enough to have questioned before becoming certain. The question then, Warren felt, was *What could have caused an unreproducible phenomenon?*

After all, Warren was in his own house. He had lived there for over twenty years. The house was old and, therefore, had certain defects, as all older houses do, but none could explain the situation. Warren would have known of any that could have.

Nor did Warren think anyone could have played a prank on him. Besides being unable to imagine what mechanism could have been used to accomplish the feat, Warren didn't see how anyone could have got in without him being aware of it. As convenient as such an explanation would have been, it just wasn't probable.

Warren felt he could only come to one conclusion. If a rational explanation didn't exist, the explanation must be irrational. A miracle had occurred.

It did not occur to Warren that the miracle was utterly insignificant, however inexplicable it was. Warren's life was too insignificant as it was; he craved significance.

What did the bath water's reversal mean? Surely even otherworldly phenomenon did not happen without some sort of reason. It had to have been a sign of some kind, revealing some secret insight of some sort or another. Warren doubted that the universe just hiccupped once in a while.

Didn't situations like that happen to saints? Warren couldn't be positive, but he thought he remembered something like that. He hadn't been raised in a particularly religious household so he couldn't remember exactly, but he did remember hearing a story or two. Didn't it have something to do with saints being holy? Perhaps that somehow gave them a negative mass, since mass was worldly.

Or, maybe it was that saints didn't rot after they died. Warren couldn't figure out if he was confusing the two situations or if he'd actually heard both. The former didn't make much sense, as no one would be able to know a saint until after he or she was already dead. That seemed silly. Warren bet the water thing was a similar situation at least.

Maybe it was a sign from God. Maybe Warren was called and that was why it only happened once. It seemed a bit vague as a sign, but Warren decided it was probably a bad idea to ignore a sign of any kind. That never seemed to go well in the Bible.

Still, Warren felt it was best not to assume he was exactly saint level. He tried to be a good person, for the most part, but he admitted he had his failings. When the grocery store clerk missed charging him for an item, he didn't call attention to it. He certainly got angry at people from time to time. No, he wasn't exactly saintly.

Warren perked up as the last few thoughts raced through his head. He did sometimes get mad when people did things the wrong way. Maybe the water was a sign that he was a prophet and should not have been staying quiet all that time. Maybe he was supposed to be telling people when they did things wrong.

He wasn't sure, but the math added up. A prophet call would explain why the water incident only happened once. If he'd been a saint, then it would have been caused by his inherent properties and happened all the time. A prophet could have just been indicated once, not being something within him. According to Warren's flawed reasoning, it added up.

Shrugging, he figured he'd give it a shot and see. He had the next day off anyway. He'd give propheting a try and see how it went. If it felt right, then he'd know. On the other hand, if it didn't, he'd know that as well and could work things out further. It didn't seem any worse a way to waste a day off than watching *Good Times* marathons or doing his taxes. What did he have to lose?

The next morning, Warren ate a bowl of plain oatmeal while he pondered how he would act out his new role. Normally he took oatmeal with plenty of butter and brown sugar, but he imagined prophets lived a more austere lifestyle—castigated themselves by doing things like going without luxuries such as butter and brown sugar.

He also thought that he should wear something a bit more prophet appropriate than his usual slacks and button up shirts. Didn't prophets usually wear sackcloth? That seemed right to Warren. Unfortunately, he didn't know what sackcloth was. He was fairly certain, regardless of exactly what it was, that he didn't have any.

Was burlap sackcloth? Warren wondered. It was a cloth that people used to make sacks. Not so often in modernly times, but certainly in the past. He wasn't sure if people had burlap in biblical times, but sackcloth had to be something close at least.

Of course, Warren didn't have burlap either. He didn't exactly have much use for it on most days. However, he did have some cushions in the basement from an old couch he'd got rid of. They were covered in a seventies sort of scratchy fabric, plain squares of white and various shades of brown. That was a bit like burlap. Regardless, it was going to have to do.

Warren ripped the covers from the cushions into big, flat rectangles and then stapled them all together. The result looked somewhat like a sleeping bag. With holes for his arms and head, it worked well enough as a makeshift prophet poncho. It may not have been traditional, but Warren figured the Lord would understand.

He put it on and left the house.

Out of modesty considerations, Warren decided to wear his prophet suit over his normal clothes. He didn't completely trust those staples to hold. Besides, the fabric really was pretty scratchy.

As Warren walked, he decided that the Market Street bus station was a decent place to begin his propheting career. It was close and might have a good amount of people. Unlike the 16th Street mall, it was enclosed, so Warren could be heard. Also, since he usually took the train to work, no one would likely remember him when it came time for his Monday commute if events didn't go well. Again, he was sure the Lord would accept that.

As Warren rode the escalator down from the street into the station, he noticed people beginning to stare. Perhaps he was projecting a prophet-aura that drew attention to him. Of course, it could also have been the fact that he was wearing a poncho made out of couch cushion covers. But, Warren figured, it didn't matter which; he'd need attention of one sort or another if he was going to be a prophet success.

There was a good crowd, lots of people to listen to Warren's holy message. Even for a Saturday, people milled about everywhere and waited in long lines for buses. It was time for Warren to get started.

The station didn't have benches. Instead, wide cement cylinders sat squat on the floor for people to rest upon. One of them was empty. Warren thought it would work marvelously as a stage, since an actual stage was not to be had. It was only a foot and a half tall or so, but that seemed like plenty.

Warren jumped atop the cylinder and shouted, "People."

Everyone turned to look at him, those who weren't already staring. However, just as Warren was about to continue, an alert about suspicious bags blared over the station PA system, drowning out Warren's voice. He waited, everyone patiently staring until the announcement completed.

"People," he again shouted. He readied himself to shout his actual message, but unfortunately, it was at that moment Warren realized he didn't have anything particular to say. He had nothing to shout.

People continued to stare.

Sure, people did things sometimes that made Warren upset. However, he wasn't mad about any of those things right then. He tried to think of what prophets usually warned against, but all of that had been said before. He wouldn't have been called to deliver redundant messages. Fornication? False idols? Already done. If people still needed to be told then they probably weren't going to listen anyway.

Besides, most of the Old Testament material didn't worry Warren very much. As long as people were decent to one another, he figured they could get whatever fun out of each other that they wanted—presuming they were adults and no one was forced. As for idols, it all seemed like different faces of the same thing to Warren. He just didn't feel that any of that was what he was supposed to talk about. He definitely wasn't going to rant about eating shellfish.

But what then? He needed to say something. The whole prophet thing hinged on delivering some message. Besides, they were all still waiting expectantly.

Warren's attention drifted to a line of people walking to the escalators. Two suits were walking much slower than the line behind them, chatting. Suddenly the two paused, for no apparent reason other than they weren't apparently in a rush and enjoyed their conversation. The line nearly bumped into them and then angrily went around, but the suits didn't appear to notice. Suddenly, Warren was angry.

"People," Warren shouted again. "Don't become so lost in your own lives that you forget that others live. It's rude. Be courteous and think of those around you. You aren't the only ones walking on sidewalks and such—so don't act like you are. Make way for others when you have no reason not to, as you would have them make way for you."

As he harangued the crowd, Warren saw that the people were actually listening to him. They were listening. They were paying attention to him. Granted, some of them, if not many of them, were laughing, but still.

It was happening. He was a prophet. He'd interpreted the sign correctly. He knew at that moment what he was to do with the rest of his life.

However, Warren realized that he was also hungry. It had been a while since his bowl of plain oatmeal. It seemed to be somewhere around lunchtime and he decided that was enough propheting for one day.

He hopped down from the cylinder. Some people clapped as Warren walked off and rode the escalator back up to the street, but some just went back to doing what they'd been doing before. That was fine, Warren was more concerned at that moment with getting himself a bowl of udon.

Warren again reflected on his fortunate choice of Market Street station; his usual udon source was a Japanese restaurant across the street. Perhaps it was coincidence, but it might have been another sign, that one validating his instincts. In any case, lunch was going to be convenient.

Several cars honked as Warren crossed the street. Likely, that was because he crossed in the middle of the busy street, as many people often did, instead of at the intersection. However, Warren also considered that his prophet suit might not have been helping matters. He pulled off the poncho, rolled it up under his arm, and went inside.

Besides, he didn't want to do any propheting during lunch. His public time was over for the day; the suit would just confuse people, make them expect things. It was best to take it off once he was off the clock. Again, he reflected on the wisdom of his choice to wear clothing underneath.

He found a private table and ordered his udon.

Normally, Warren did not consider himself to be particularly adventurous food-wise. His tastes were pretty simple for the most part, oatmeal, sandwiches, hamburgers, roast, and all that sort of standard thing. American food.

For some reason, though, he'd picked up a penchant for udon after reading about it in a Murakami novel. Noodle soup, long and thick udon noodles, broth, and so forth. Usually a few green onions. Sometimes chicken and sometimes seafood. In most cases, which should be all cases in Warren's opinion, a fish cake would sit on top.

Warren wasn't sure why it was called a fish cake. There was no bread. It was nothing like a crab cake; it was a floppy white fish disk, usually dyed pink around the edge with a dot of pink dye in the center, about the size of a Kennedy half dollar and twice as thick—though considerably floppier.

The fish cake was Warren's favorite part of udon, though he really didn't care too much for the taste. It delighted him to merely see the fish cake on top of the bowl and he loved to look at it. It was the most important part. However, it was kind of rubbery and the flavor was off-putting. It was a jewel, an ornament, and it's intended purpose was somewhat beside the point.

Although, he did always eat it. It was just that eating the fish cake never made him quite as happy as merely looking at it. Still, the meal wasn't complete if he left if behind.

The udon arrived and the waiter backed away after setting the large, wide bowl on Warren's table. Fortunately, the customary fish cake was present, sitting atop the broth. The udon smelled delicious, particularly since Warren was likely smelling the broth as opposed to the fish cake.

Though Warren enjoyed udon a little spicy, he had not ordered it that way. At this particular restaurant, spicy was accomplished by the inclusion of dried red pepper flakes. That functioned, but the flakes never integrated well with the soup as a whole and tended to catch in Warren's throat.

Personally, Warren preferred to add the chili paste that was always present on the table in a clear plastic bottle with a green spout. He never remembered what it was called, but it had a white rooster on the side.

He grabbed the chili paste bottle and squirted a liberal amount over the bowl. Then he grabbed the chopsticks from the table and stirred the paste into the soup. Warren knew this could end up cooling the soup a bit, but udon was usually served hot enough that this was not a significant problem.

Warren watched the udon as he stirred. The fish cake submerged and the fat coils of wheat noodles undulated and swarmed like sightless sea serpents. He stirred, and stirred, waiting for the chili paste to mix uniformly. The noodles continued to roll. However, the fish cake did not resurface.

Warren frowned. If the fish cake wasn't on the surface, then he couldn't look at it. That wasn't any good; it removed the whole point of having the fish cake. He stirred some more, but couldn't locate the cake.

He figured it must have got caught up in all the noodles. There were an awful lot of noodles, after all. He just started eating them, grabbing a cluster into the air to let them cool and then slurping them into his mouth, figuring that was the most efficient way to locate the missing cake.

However, he eventually reached the end of the noodles and had found no sign of the fish cake. He continued to stir but located nothing. The fish cake, no longer possibly encumbered by noodles, should have easily floated to the top.

Still, there was a great deal of broth remaining and Warren couldn't see through it very well. Warren thought the fish cake must have just taken on too much liquid and ceased being able to float. That didn't make a whole lot of sense to him, given that the cake was all rubbery fish and not soggy bread, thusly not likely to take on any liquid at all, but it was the only explanation Warren could think of. It must have just been poor luck that he hadn't managed to stir it to the surface. Though, again, there was an awful lot of broth.

So, Warren started in on the broth. He'd find the cake sooner or later and could at least look at it for a little bit then before finishing. He grabbed the wide plastic oriental spoon that had been brought with the udon and shoveled broth into his mouth.

His heart sank, though, as he reached the bottom of the bowl without finding anything. The bowl was empty at that point and Warren could deny the situation no longer. His fish cake was gone.

Warren wondered briefly if he could have accidentally eaten it, unaware while slurping the broth and noodles. He shook his head, though. That just wasn't possible. He'd been too careful, too watching. He would have known the very item for which he was looking so hard. Besides, that taste was unmistakable. He would have known it anywhere.

He also pondered if all his stirring might not have broken up the cake so that it disappeared into the broth, but that didn't work either. Even if it had happened, contrary to the fact that it had never happened before, the whole bowl would have tasted of it. There was no way he could have missed fish cake flavored udon. And, more importantly, it hadn't tasted like that.

No, the fish cake had simply disappeared. Warren wondered where it could possibly have gone and how.

Amidst all of this, Warren neglected to wonder whether or not he should really care.

Did someone steal it? Did it travel through time? Or could it have gone to another dimension?

Even if the cake had been stolen, Warren thought it could not have been accomplished through normal physical means. He would have seen, of this he was certain. Whatever had occurred, it had to have been something *beyond*. Another miracle.

Warren had to find out. He had to investigate. This was clearly more miraculous than sinking bath water, Warren decided this was the unexplained disappearance of actual matter. Plainly, this took precedence and any prophet stuff would just have to wait. The fact that a missing fish cake was about as meaningless as missing bath water escaped Warren's notice.

"Excuse me," Warren called to the waiter. "My fish cake is missing."

The waiter shuffled over. He looked in the bowl. "I'm very sorry, sir. Perhaps we missed that. I could get another if you like?"

"No," Warren explained patiently. "The fish cake itself doesn't matter, it's that it disappeared."

The waiter pursed his lips. Warren decided the waiter thought Warren was mistaken, that Warren had eaten it without noticing. Perhaps he even thought Warren was lying to get a free fish cake. The waiter was going to be no help at all.

"Pardon me," Warren said to the two girls at the table next to his, "have you by any chance seen my fish cake?"

The girls gawked at him, "Ummm. No," they finally answered. Then they turned away and giggled hysterically.

Frustrated, Warren stood up. "People, please. Does anyone know what happened to my fish cake? This is very important. It vanished off the face of the earth. I need help."

Some unpleasantness followed after that. More than one person had mumbled *you sure do* and Warren became a bit agitated. In the end, he was allowed to leave without payment by way of apology for the fish cake. That was nice and all, but Warren didn't want an apology. He wanted to find out what had happened.

As he walked home from the restaurant, Warren contemplated how he should proceed. Asking around hadn't got him anywhere. He guessed that he would just have to expand his search.

Should he post flyers around town? Perhaps he could take out an ad on craigslist, *Fish cake vanished. Reward for information.* He could even hire a private detective. If someone out there knew what had happened, then he needed to find them and make them talk. If no one knew, well, he'd take that from there. At the very least, he desperately needed to know more than he did at that moment.

Warren rubbed his chin and thought as he crossed an empty street. He looked both ways to make sure it was clear, but a black Smart Car zipped out of nowhere as he crossed and nearly struck him as it whooshed past. He felt the rush of wind even before he heard the tiny honk. Startled, he could only stare as it careened down the street and out of sight.

Where had it come from? Warren was sure that the Smart Car had not been there the moment before; he had checked. It had just suddenly appeared, blasting past with full momentum.

He paused. Had he perhaps just looked by way of habit without really paying attention? He didn't think so. He remembered actually looking. Had the Smart Car been traveling so fast that it hadn't been there when he looked and suddenly was a moment later? That wasn't likely, given that it was a Smart Car.

No, it had to have suddenly materialized in full motion. Out of nowhere.

Warren swallowed. This made odd bath water and straying fish cakes seem frivolous to Warren, who did not see how equally miraculous and trivial the three events were in comparison with each other. This was a far darker sort of miracle, a miracle that might very well be out to kill him, dangerous miracles that could come out of anywhere, at any time, to strike him down. Still, it hadn't killed him. There was that.

Warren futilely wondered *What did it all mean?*

THE UNKNOWABLE AGENDA OF
URSINES

It wasn't like I'd never seen a bear before, but I guess things are different in the bar at a casino. Not in a cage or anything, just a bear walking in like he did it every day. I'd certainly never seen that.

There was just me and the bartender in there. I'd been parked on that stool long enough, nursing beers and listening to the beeps and whistles of slot machines, that the bartender wasn't even making polite small talk anymore. She was just washing out glasses waitresses brought in from the casino and left me on my own. That was all right, though. It was payday again and I was just playing the same game I did every two weeks.

Honey, I thought to the waitress as I pretended to be the aging ex-marine, *decking yourself out in a tip-getting tube top ain't gonna get you nowhere. It's been a few years since anybody was willing to tip to see them saggy cans.*

For some reason, whenever I sat in that bar I kept imagining myself as a white trash retiree ex-marine. Really, I wasn't even thirty yet and was more Cherokee than anything else, but I guess I felt that's who should drink at that bar.

I had a decent enough gig teaching at the community college up the road, but on what it paid I'd never repay the forty grand it'd taken me to get in there. Every payday I'd get the big idea that I'd screw everything. Take my check to the casino and win enough to be free of it all. But I'd just sit in the crappy little bar, trying to get up my nerve, until reality set in and I slunk home to pay bills. Things were about to that point again, like normal. Course, *normally* it didn't involve the bear.

"Honey," I shouted at the bartender in my out-loud aging ex-marine voice, shaking my empty bottle. "I'm drier than a two dollar whore's cooch over here. Help out a hardworking American."

The bartender didn't seem to care. She cracked another bottle from the cooler and slammed it down in front of me. Didn't even pick up the old empty.

That's when the bear walked in.

Now, I don't mean on all fours, or riding a unicycle and juggling. Two legs, like the grizzly was human. Dressed in baggy denim overalls, a red Pendleton shirt, and a green seed cap. He shambled over and sat down on the stool next to me.

"What'll you have?" the bartender asked, either not noticing or not caring that it was a bear. I guess she served all kinds. She put a beer in front of him when he pointed a claw at mine.

I sat there, trying not to look at the bear. Didn't even drink off my beer. It seemed like I should do something, but I'd never thought of how I might respond to that kind of situation. The bear drank his beer, however, and he managed that without any thumbs.

"So," I said, deciding to stay with the aging ex-marine shtick, "it true what they say 'bout the woods?"

"Yup," he rasped. "The Pope craps there and I'm Catholic." He took a pull off his bottle. "Now cut the shit, Stan, this ain't a social call."

I looked up at the bartender, but she wasn't paying any mind so I looked back at the bear. The bear that somehow knew my name. "I know you, fella?"

The bear flexed his claws. I couldn't tell if he was menacing me or if he was just stretching. "Couple weeks ago. Up at the campground."

I remembered, not that I had really forgotten. Heck, how could I forget? I was out for a little fresh air and some crazy bear jumped onto the back of my car. He fell off when I floored it, but my car got pretty scratched up.

"That was you?" I edged away. "You'll excuse me if I didn't recognize you." Maybe he'd come to finish me off, not that a bear carrying out a vendetta was even remotely possible. Clearly, I'd lost my marbles and was hallucinating.

"Yup, me." He took a pull off his beer before wiping his snout with a huge paw. "I got to thinking, how many people escape a bear attack like that? How many even have a bear jump on their car? You've got to have some amazing luck, or maybe we've got some universe-connection. Either way, I figured we had to put it to work at the tables. And then I find out you're already in a casino."

Luck? How was getting attacked by a bear luck? Even if I got away. I finally managed to remember my beer and drank. "How'd you find that out?"

The bear shrugged. "I know things."

I checked to see what the bartender thought of all this, but she still wasn't paying any attention. Maybe I was just crazy. Maybe this insane conversation wasn't happening at all. Seemed like this should have piqued her interest in some way if it was real. Then I relaxed. Being crazy was safer than sitting with a bear that had already demonstrated a desire to knock a piece off me.

"You want me to gamble with you? You tried to kill me."

The bear waved a paw at me. "Aww, I'm done with all that. We've got other business now. However," the bear growled, displaying his claws in an unambiguously alarming fashion, "if you aren't down, we can always go back to the other."

I swallowed. I felt myself sweating even though the bar had the air up so high the drinks didn't need ice to stay cool. I might have been crazy, but it was probably better to do what the bear said— just in case.

"Right then," the bear said. "Let's get to it." He downed his beer and slid off the stool, looking back at me to do the same.

I took my beer with me, but other than that I tried not to anger the bear and complied. The bartender showed no concern that her only patrons were leaving. She just collected the empties before cutting some lemons. I realized as we walked off, or shambled in the case of the bear, that she hadn't even cared enough to make us pay.

As I followed the bear into the actual casino itself, the clanging and dinging of the slot machines got louder. Course, the casino was just one giant warehouse sort of room, so I'm sure it all echoed a bit. The only separation was different games grouped together. Two main sections, one for slots and the other for table games. Different denominations and varieties formed little neighborhoods. Still, it was all one united gambling city. Only the bar was off in another room, a suburb.

"I'm partial to roulette," I offered.

The bear continued purposefully as if he hadn't heard. Then again, maybe he hadn't. I didn't think bears were used to casinos, all the flashing lights and changing noises. Not that I was used to it either, since I usually hung out at the bar. Anyway, I thought maybe the background noise made it too hard to keep track of everything and I could slip out unnoticed.

Before I acted on that, though, the bear stopped at the high-stakes blackjack table. Five-hundred-dollar-minimum. He nodded to the empty chair in front of the uninterested dealer.

"Umm. . . this is a bit out of my price range."

The balding fat-ass of a dealer stared across the casino as if we weren't there, not even bothering to acknowledge our presence with a glance. He obviously knew I didn't belong there.

"Trust me," the bear snarled, bearing some seriously yellowed fangs. He dragged a chair out with a muscled paw. "This one's just right."

Needing no further threats, I quickly sat down. The bear sat as well. He seemed to slouch, but I couldn't really be sure. Maybe bears just sat like that.

"Are the gentlemen aware of the minimum?" the dealer snorted, apparently not worried about bears.

"Just watching," the bear grunted. "This here's your player. Place a bet, Stan."

"Me?" Five hundred? That was about all I'd got paid that morning.

The bear put a massive paw on my shoulder. It looked friendly, but I could feel those claws. "Hey, only you can prevent forest fires."

I reluctantly dropped my money on the table, relieved when the claws withdrew. The dealer snatched my money away, far too quickly for my tastes, with some little stick thing.

"Changing five hundred," he muttered, shoving my money in a little slot, never to be seen again I was sure and dropped a few chips in front of me. Obviously, he thought this would be over quick.

Next, the dealer tossed me a card and dealt himself one. Mine was a nine and his was a ten. Then he tossed me another nine before dealing himself another card, face down this time.

"Hit him," the bear said.

"What? I've got eighteen. You'll bust me. I'd be crazy to hit now."

The bear just looked at me. "Crazy enough to fight a bear?" It seemed like his eyebrow raised, but I couldn't tell if he had eyebrows or not.

"I guess not," I mumbled, nodding at the dealer. Better in the red than dead.

But then the dealer tossed me a three. I stared at it as if it might start talking to me as well. It wouldn't have been any more of a surprise; I'd already come to terms with the fact that a bear was forcing me to risk all my money on blackjack.

"Stay," I whispered.

The dealer turned over his card—another ten. I had to remember to breathe as the dealer dealt himself another card. It was a third ten.

"House busts," the dealer sneered, tossing some more chips in front of me.

Somehow, some way I couldn't even grasp, it'd all worked out. I wasn't broke and I wasn't maimed. Definitely the best-case scenario. I found myself starting to hope that the bear was real and I wasn't seeing things after all.

I almost snatched the chips as a matter of reflex, but I stopped myself just short. The bear hadn't said not to, but he hadn't got up yet either. He was just watching me.

"Another hand?" I asked.

"If you're smarter than the average bear," he yawned and shrugged. I'm guessing he knew I was on board by that point.

"Again," I said to the dealer.

"Goody."

The dealer's attitude seemed to change as I won the next hand, and the next one, and the one after that. As the chip pile got bigger, more of his comments ended with *sir*.

At some point, the bear stretched and got up. "Well, hibernation calls. This old bear is tuckered out."

I almost protested, but then I saw the bear's glance at a suit nearby, a guy with a wire leading to something in his ear. He was very obvious about not watching us, as very obviously as he apparently could. I took the hint.

"Guess I should probably stick to the bear necessities, too," I joked, scooping the chips into an improvised sack made with the front of my shirt. "Quit while I'm ahead,"

The bear walked off. I had to hurry to grab all the chips and catch up. He wasn't waiting for me to follow, though. He walked right out of the casino.

"Wait," I called, catching up in the gravel parking lot outside. "Let me cash these in and get you your share. There's got to be fifty thousand here at least. You deserve at least half or more."

The bear turned. "What the hell am I going to do with money? I'm a damn bear," he snorted and shambled off toward the woods at the end of the lot. "Tell you what, though," he grunted back at me, "bring some food next time you go to a campground. Some fucking sandwiches at least."

THE HEADSHAKING DISAPPOINTMENT
OF THE MISGUIDEDLY WELL-
INTENTIONED

Home was a piece-of-crap high-rise downtown. Brookview Tower four. It wasn't run down or anything, but it was a group of late-seventies tall box constructions. Cheap and dull. Also, downtown there was neither views nor brooks, let alone views of brooks. Still, the rent was as cheap as the construction, and it was close to campus.

I lived on the fourteenth floor, so I definitely got in one of the elevators. There probably had to be stairs somewhere in order to satisfy fire codes, but I wouldn't have known one way or another. I got in, pushed the button for my floor, and waited as the door closed and the elevator started to rise.

I just about pissed myself when I realized I wasn't alone in there.

I happened to glance to my left and almost screamed. There was a guy all crouched down, hiding at the back of the elevator, hands spread out to the adjacent walls like he was bracing himself, twitching like he was going to pop, pupils as big and dark as overripe Bing cherries. He was terrified. I was terrified. We were both trapped in that little metal box, way too close to each other.

I'm guessing he was a meth-head; he looked pretty strung out. Greasy brown hair with a receding hairline, bad skin, Lynyrd Skynyrd T-shirt with the sleeves ripped off, acid wash Wranglers, and three-day-old lawn crew funk; it all fit. There was also the fact that he looked like a mouse caught in the middle of a kitchen floor when someone suddenly turned the light on. Yeah, he was probably in the midst of a gigantic freak-out at that moment—

totally tweaked. He kept flinching like I was going to jump him, even though I hadn't moved.

I stared straight ahead as if I didn't even see him. I was sure he was going to leap on me and start chewing my face. Pinned in there with a panicked tweaker, I pretended I was alone. The moment the doors popped open, I bolted and rushed for my apartment door.

On the other side, with the deadbolt secure and my pulse slowing to normal, I calmed down enough to think about how odd the whole thing had been. The poor meth-head must have wandered in off the street by accident and when the elevator door opened, he must have instinctively gone inside. Then he was stuck. Heck, it seemed like he'd probably starve in there. He'd obviously done all right up until then, but I was sure he wouldn't be able to get out on his own. It'd be a slow death.

It seemed cruel to let him die alone in that elevator. He'd suffer, unable to do anything to help himself. He must have had a family once. Maybe he'd even been a good guy, back when he still had a working brain. I imagined the pain and fear he was going to feel as he was stuck in there longer and longer, yearning to be free. Burned out as he was, I was pretty sure he could still feel pain. It hurt to see anything suffer.

But, maybe I was overreacting. Maybe he'd been surprised to find me in there with him and then snuck out again right after. Maybe I was getting all worked up over nothing. I really didn't have a whole lot of experience with meth-heads.

Telling myself to be brave, I walked out into the hall and pressed the elevator button.

No, he was still in there when the elevator door opened. He was still there and he was still cowering at the back, trying to be as small and unnoticeable as he could be. For some reason, he didn't seem scary anymore. I'd probably been startled the first time. I got in and pushed the button for the first floor.

I didn't feel trapped that time, sealed in there as the elevator descended. I tried to think how I was going to get the meth-head out of there. Picking him up would have been easiest, but he was so scared that he'd probably scratch or bite me. He wouldn't have been trying to hurt me, but he was too panicked to be safe.

The elevator doors opened before I'd managed to think of a plan. Crap. We both kind of stood there, him crouching. I started feeling like a pretty big tool. He was probably still feeling terrified.

"Shoo!" I yelled at him finally.

He flinched.

"Shoo." I motioned at the open door. "Go on. Get out of here."

He looked at me.

Finally, the elevator doors started to close again and I stepped out into the lobby. I needed time to think about getting him out. The elevator didn't seem like the best place to do that, too much pressure.

I thought about calling animal control. They probably had more experience with that sort of thing, meth-heads stuck in elevators and all. I thought they'd know how to do it safely. But there was a big chance that they'd call the police or something like that. I didn't want to get the poor guy in trouble. No, it seemed like it was best for me to handle it on my own.

I got the elevator open again. I thought maybe if I turned the light out in there and held the door, then he'd follow the light into the lobby and on out again. That way I wouldn't have to touch him. All animals went toward the light, right? He'd know which way was outside again and act on it.

However, that was easier said, or thought, than done. The elevator didn't have a freight setting or a stop switch, so I had to wedge one of my shoes in the door to keep it open. The other I just held onto, since it was weird trying to walk with just one shoe. Also, when the door stayed open too long, a really loud, annoying buzzer went off. I don't think it was helping the meth-head's calm any.

Worse, there wasn't any easy way to turn off the light. There certainly wasn't a switch; I looked. I had to try to climb up so I could reach the ceiling, pull down the plastic sheets covering the light, and unscrew the bulbs. Luckily, there was at least a handrail around the middle of the elevator I could stand on though it wasn't very wide. I had to get up on that, pushing off the adjacent elevator wall to stay up, and reach for the ceiling. With no shoes. With the buzzer blaring the whole time. With the meth-head basically crapping himself while all that was going on.

Still, I did get the light out. It was kind of nice in there, dark and cozy with the light creeping in from the lobby. I thought for sure the meth-head would calm down and start to wander out. I was pretty proud of myself.

Of course, he didn't end up going anywhere.

Maybe it was too cozy. It was kind of cave-like, after all. Maybe he finally felt safe and didn't want to leave. Maybe he never wanted to go outside at all. All I know for sure is that he sat there. I waited, hanging on to the side of the elevator like I was, for a really long time.

At one point, some cute short girl dressed in a black tank top and what looked like white pajama bottoms with pink polka dots walked up to get in the elevator. She froze when she saw me clinging to the side of the elevator and the meth-head crouched in the corner. I don't know if the light being out made things worse. She turned and walked away.

Great. The whole building was going to think I was nuts.

Worse, distracted by the girl, that was when I dropped my other shoe. It hit the floor of the elevator and bounced over in the corner with the meth-head. There was no way I'd be able to get that back without moving him first.

I was getting a bit pissed off. My legs were cramping and my toes were going numb. I'd had to tuck them into the railing to get any leverage. I was really starting to care a lot less if I hurt the guy to get him out of there. Humanitarian impulses aside, I wanted my shoes back. I was about ready to grab him and pull.

Still, I wasn't quite licked. I had to clean up the mess first, but I did have an idea. I replaced the bulbs so I'd be able to see, got down, reclaimed the shoe I could get without risking a meth-head attack, and rode the elevator back up to my apartment.

It took me a while of searching to find *it*. I remembered buying one, but it had been a while and I didn't know if I'd thrown it out. There were any number of places I could have put it. It wasn't like I'd ever really found a need for the thing. Finally, I found it in the old box from my PlayStation at the back of my closet. Then I marched back down the hall and got right back in the elevator.

I think the meth-head realized something was up; he looked over at me. He was still freaking, but there was a watchful wariness in his pulsating eyes. I smiled at him like he was someone else's kid sitting next to me alone on a bus. The ride down was uneventful. The doors opened again on the lobby. Then I took *it* out of my pocket. Not being completely incompetent, I wore my earplugs.

"*BUWWWAAAH,*" the air horn in my hand blared.

The meth-head really lost it then. He jumped and crouched, gibbered and spat. I thought his eyes were going to explode. He screamed, and squeaked, and thrashed, and flinched all at the same time.

"*BUUUAWWWWWAAAAHHH!*" It sounded again as I pressed it a second time. An air horn is really loud in an elevator, even with the door open.

At that, the meth-head burst out into the lobby. He ran and didn't look back. He ran out of the elevator, into the lobby, and out of the building.

I'd done it; I'd managed to get him out. My shoes were mine again.

Of course, he ran right out into traffic and got hit by a speeding bus. My building is downtown, after all. More importantly, there's a really busy street out front and the meth-head got flattened like a pancake. Guess I hadn't thought things through quite that far. Probably would have been better if I'd left the guy alone.

My bad.

UP, UP, AND NO WAY

Chuck knew that the blind date was over when the girl asked him whether, if for some reason he had the choice, he'd choose the ability to fly or to become invisible. It wasn't that he was offended by the question, just that he knew she wouldn't like the answer he had to give.

"Invisible," he said and watched her heavily makeup-covered face scrunch up in disapproval.

He signaled for the waitress to bring their check. The date was doubtlessly unsalvageable at that point. Chuck figured he might as well start preparing for exit.

Up until that moment, he thought things had been going pretty well. The girl was a little flighty, but she was friendly and fairly attractive even despite the excessive makeup. They'd gone to an Ethiopian restaurant he was fond of. The food was good there and eating with little bits of the pancake-like bread instead of silverware tended to create a fun atmosphere for first dates. However, Chuck saw that was all ejected when she asked him the question.

"Invisible? Are you some kind of voyeur pervert or something?"

Chuck didn't answer. He just chewed a bit of lamb stew and waited for her to go on. No sense in letting the food go to waste.

Admittedly, he had certainly known better. It was one of those idiotic questions that supposedly revealed your personality. People who chose flying were dreamers; they longed to be free, to soar. Invisibles, on the other hand, were sinister deviants. They wanted to cheat and steal, violate others.

After all, there was no *honest* use for invisibility. The only thing you could do with it was hide. Really, it was even only for small-time deviants. You could use it to shoplift, but really valuable items, like those that would be stored in the vault of a bank, were secured well enough that you'd need more than just not to be seen. It worked best for creeps who wanted to watch women change in locker rooms.

"I'd definitely fly," the effusive girl went on. Chuck was almost sure her name was Heather, but he hadn't known her long enough to memorize it. At that point, he doubted he'd have any need to do so in the future. It was just another setup organized by well-meaning friends.

"Think of all the things you could do, go anywhere at any time. I'd see the world; I'd see it as no other person gets to see it."

Chuck continued chewing. He knew what she'd do. It wasn't like he hadn't thought of all that. These weren't exactly startling insights. The girl was probably not going to be much of a loss, particularly since she seemed to think he had never thought of those things.

She gushed in that vein for a while after that, but eventually clammed up when she saw that Chuck wasn't following too closely. He didn't feel bad; the opinion she'd formed of him from his choice was a deal breaker anyway. After that, she'd just wanted to be able to talk without concern for who was listening. She was playing, letting the dream of flying feel real for a moment, and she didn't really involve Chuck in any of it.

They finished the meal in silence. Then Chuck paid the bill and they left, separately once they were outside. It was a little awkward when they finally broke to go in different directions, but each clearly wanted to go and they both mumbled, "this was nice," without any reference to future plans or even a later call.

On his solitary car ride home, Chuck wondered if he should have just lied. He hadn't felt like lying, though, when he didn't even know whether or not it was worth it to get close to her. Since his answer was going to be wrong in any event, he figured there was nothing to really lose.

Of course, he had never actually wanted to be invisible. It was simply the only answer he could choose. He could already fly, and that hadn't ever worked out too well.

Flight had first come as a dream, one that he remembered portions of vividly even though the rest had vanished the moment he woke. He'd been some kind of wizard talking to a fat crone in a crowded wooden shack reminiscent of an old garden shed. There had been some tiny animated clay man in a little chair on a table, obviously in agony, defecating endlessly. The sight filled Chuck with revulsion and an unexplained desire to die.

He had left the hut and the golem. There was some a girl he needed to save. Grabbing her around her slim waist, her delicate arms wrapped needfully around his shoulders, he let something surge within him. He felt filled with power and that power shot through him, propelling him, and the raven-haired girl with him, from the ground and into the sky.

For some reason, it felt like surfing on the blast of a rushing wave. However, he'd never surfed before. He knew he had no way of knowing if that was how surfing felt, but that was how he felt.

The weirdest part was when he woke up. He swore that he fell onto his bed, as if he'd been levitating and then suddenly plummeted a couple of inches. Dreams could be like that, though, he figured as his mind returned. The body creates the sensation of falling and the arms reflexively smack the mattress to stop it, making it seem like an actual fall.

Chuck decided that was all it had been and went back to sleep.

However, later, that feeling of power coursing through his body as he flew in the dream. It had felt so real, so right. He wanted to feel that way again.

The memory of that moment replayed over and over in his mind. Even though it was just pretend, really, Chuck let himself give in to it. If the sensation wasn't real, he figured he might as well enjoy the thought of it. Thinking still managed to feel like something was coursing through him. Power. Joy. Exultation.

Suddenly, Chuck's feet lifted off the ground.

Chuck was floored. Or rather, he was actually the opposite. He rose into the air. His feet were completely disconnected from the ground. He could fly. He could actually fly.

That was the moment that it all went bad.

In the second that Chuck was filled with ecstasy, a horrifying panic crushed in from all sides. Cut from direct connection with the earth, his mind pictured the planet's overwhelming immensity. It seemed to get bigger and bigger while he shrunk smaller and smaller next to it. The immense bulk would swallow him whole. He'd be pulled in by its terrible proximity and ground to dust like a gnat.

His stomach clenched and his skin went cold. He was going to vomit. Everything started to spin terribly around him. He was lost forever without any ability to even tell which way was up. He wanted to die. He *wanted* to *die*.

Then Chuck did throw up.

His feet were suddenly back on the ground. Wracked with breathless, gasping sobs, his body convulsed. There was vomit all down his front. It stunk.

And yet, he was peaceful again. All the horror left and Chuck didn't know where it had gone. The only thing he knew was how wonderful it felt for the other feeling to be gone.

That's when he tried to fly again.

That's when the other feeling immediately returned.

As Chuck cleaned the wet sick off of himself, he managed to finally think clearly enough to grasp the situation. He had the power to fly, but not the ability. Every time he tried, the fear would pounce on him. The harder he tried to overcome it, the more crushing the fear became. Chuck was helpless.

He was ashamed. One of the most marvelous gifts ever given to a human being had been given to him, and he was too afraid to use it. He was a coward. He was a coward and the gift was wasted.

There was nothing more he wanted at that moment than to use his power to fly. It wasn't even the actual flying that he cared about that much. That would have been wonderful, even though he'd never pined for flight specifically. It was more that it had been granted to him and he couldn't make himself do it. Plainly, he felt guilty.

He felt that guilt again, as he often had since discovering his power, when he returned home from the date disaster. The poor result of the evening didn't bother him so much, but it dredged up flying once again. Chuck wished he could only have forgotten all about it.

He got a bottle of Black Velvet from under the kitchen sink.

Frankly, Chuck hated Black Velvet. It wasn't even one of the better-blended whiskeys, and Chuck didn't like blended whiskey at all. He preferred bourbon.

Black Velvet was for bad moods. It was for wallowing. As a whiskey, it was cheap and it tasted like it. There was a rancid yet sweet medicine taste to it that made Chuck queasy, and it almost never failed to give him heartburn the moment he started drinking.

One of his old work supervisors got him on Black Velvet, insisting it was the thing to drink—directly from the bottle—when watching *Apocalypse Now*. Chuck had to admit, though he hated the Black Velvet itself, it made him feel like he was mirroring the character in the movie when he drank it. It was unpleasant, but it was an interesting experience. He re-watched *Apocalypse Now* from time to time so he always kept a bottle handy.

It also worked when he felt like punishing himself. He'd enjoy the drunk once it came on, but he never enjoyed the actual drinking. Emotionally, for whatever reason, that little bit of self-flagellation helped. He needed it sometimes.

For example, he needed it when he got home from the date. It was just that sort of a time. He ripped off the top and took a slug of the awful stuff. The top he just tossed somewhere off into the room.

At first, Chuck drank in the semi-darkness on his couch. The only light was the small amount that got in through his window blinds from the streetlights. For a moment he imagined a ceiling fan whirring above him, which he didn't have, and sounding like a chopper. He cut that out quickly, though. That night wasn't one of his *Apocalypse Now* nights and that image wasn't the right mood at all.

He made himself drink quietly, no pretending or enjoyment. Chuck was determined not to have a good time until the booze made him. Until then, he was stewing.

His brain was still agitated, though. Eventually, as the level in the bottle progressively dropped, it started feeling right to pace. Back and forth across the room he went, swinging the bottle and putting it to his lips once in a while. He was angry, after all. He was angry at himself, but he was also angry at everything for turning out the way it had.

Pacing was good for angry drinking.

It just wasn't fair, he thought as he continued to drink and pace. The anger came easily. He was definitely getting drunk quickly. He could feel his skin buzzing with it.

That was good; indignation crowded out shame and regret.

Why was he given a power if he was also made unable to use it? It was like a *Twilight Zone* punishment, something that at first seemed sweet but actually turned out bitter. Had something done it just to mess with him? Something had to have, something with an extremely cruel sense of humor. It was too tragic to have been a coincidence. Tragedy required malice.

Was it something he was supposed to overcome and he had failed the test? Perhaps the terror only got stronger to a certain point, a point to which he'd been unable to endure, and then it would vanish? Was that what he had to do in order to fly?

Chuck sneered and nearly threw the bottle at a wall. He caught himself, though, remembering at the last moment that it still had whiskey he could drink. The whiskey wasn't what he was angry at.

Though it didn't feel like it at that moment, the chain of drunk thoughts and anger wasn't new for Chuck. In fact, he did his drunk-shtick fairly often, and each time it was almost exactly the same. It was a pattern he repeated, but it always felt spontaneous each time he resorted to it.

Of course, he didn't usually lurch into the coffee table mid-stride. He was drunker than normal and lost his balance while pacing. The cheap table flipped and the momentum of his charge threw him forward into the air. Accidentally, he let the power surge through him in order to catch himself and started to fly.

Instantly, he realized what he was doing and tried to stop. He feared the fear.

However, the booze slowed his reactions. Before he could fully stop himself, he realized that the panic had not arrived. Instead of increasingly imagining his tiny size right next to the enormity of a planet, he felt he was the enormous one. He was powerful. He was confident. The planet was the speck, not him.

Chuck reflected as best he could while he floated in midair. The alcohol invincibility trumped the feeling of being crushed. He felt he was the center of the universe so he wasn't tetherless in the empty void of space. It was only delusion, but it worked. He could finally fly and it felt incredible.

Unfortunately, Chuck was startled out of his alcohol-addled revelry to notice that he was sinking. With joy, he let the power loose for all he was worth (forgetting about the ceiling for a moment), ready to blast off into the heavens. This was no time to drift down; this was the time to soar. But, he shot nowhere. His descent accelerated until his feet were again on the floor.

Chuck was puzzled. He tried again to fly, but nothing happened. It was as if flying had just been a dream after all. No matter what he did, he could not fly.

He flopped down onto the couch. Was that it? Had he just been given the power to torment him until he figured out how to use it, whereupon it was taken back? Chuck didn't know. Regardless, at least he no longer had a gift that he was too scared to use. His power was definitely gone, but he didn't have to be ashamed anymore.

Leaning his head back on the couch armrest, Chuck passed out. The bottle of Black Velvet slipped from his hand and tumbled to the floor. The small amount of brown liquid that had still been inside leaked out and soaked into the carpet.

Chuck's head pounded as he awoke in the morning. His blinds were still closed, but the sunlight that made it inside the room burned. He rolled his dry tongue around in his sticky mouth; he could still taste the nasty sweetness of the cheap whiskey.

As his head cleared, the hangover wasn't painful enough to suppress his elation at remembering that his curse had been lifted. He was free. Not free to fly, but free in an important way nevertheless.

In celebration, Chuck got to his feet and let the power surge so he could again see it do nothing. To his shock, however, he started to rise. Just as quick, the panic leaped upon him. Immediately, he slammed himself to the ground. He grabbed onto the couch desperately as a brace, his body trembling. Eventually, he calmed enough to sit back down.

So, he thought to himself and sighed, *I can still fly.*

Chuck puzzled. He really hadn't been able to fly, he hadn't. As he thought, he wondered if being drunk had taken away his ability. It had worked at first, but then it just petered out. That was the only explanation he could think of. Since he was sober again, he could fly again.

He rubbed his eyes as he thought about how cruelly logical it all lined up. For whatever reason he knew how to fly, but was prevented from doing so by fear. Alcohol took away the fear, but also the power to fly. There was a certain humorousness to it, Chuck felt, presuming you happened to hate him or at least enjoy his suffering.

Chuck sighed again. *Oh well,* he thought, *I'm no worse off than before.*

He figured it was best not to dwell too much, disappointing though it was. Another blind date was scheduled for that night with a different girl and he needed to shake off the hangover before then.

Maybe this one wouldn't ask stupid questions. Or, if she did, maybe she'd be someone he'd care enough about to lie to.

ABOUT THE AUTHOR

David S. Atkinson's writing appears in *Bartleby Snopes, Grey Sparrow Journal, Atticus Review,* and other journals.

Not Quite So Stories is his third book.

Other books by David S. Atkinson

Bones Buried in the Dirt

The Garden of Good and Evil Pancakes

He spends his non-literary time working as a patent attorney in Denver.

davidsatkinsonwriting.com

PREVIOUS PUBLICATIONS

"Turndown Service." *The Writing Disorder,* Spring *2014.*

"Home Improvement." *Chamber Four Lit Magazine,* C4, no 4.

"Monkey! Monkey! Monkey! Monkey! Monkey!" *Wilderness House Literary Review,* Vol. 8, no. 2.

"Happy Trails." *Martian Lit,* June 10, 2013.

"Changes for the Château." *Swamp Biscuits and Tea,* May 2013, no 4.

"The Des Moines Kabuki Dinner Theatre." *Bartleby Snopes,* June 4, 2013.

"The Des Moines Kabuki Dinner Theatre." *Bartleby Snopes,* 2013, no. 10.

"Cents of Wonder Rhymes With Orange." *Thrice Fiction,* March 2013, no. 7.

"The Bricklayer's Ambiguous Morality." *The Lincoln Underground,* Spring 2013.

"The Unknowable Agenda of Ursines." *Crack the Spine,* October 16, 2012, no. 43.

"G-Men." *JMWW,* Summer 2012.

"Context Driven." *The Zodiac Review,* Spring 2012 .

"Domestic Ties." *Atticus Review,* August 30, 2011.

"Domestic Ties." *Get Lit, Round 1: Short Fiction, 2011.*